Rebecca Thompson

The Act

Imprint: Amazon
FIRST Edition
Language: English
Country: United Kingdom
Keywords: Family, Scandal, Love, Life, Death, Friendships
Licence: Standard Copyright License: ©
Copy Editor and Proofreader: Amazon KDP, Google Docs. Jessica Toft & Paul Walker
Book Cover Designer and Illustrator: Amazon KDP
Author: Rebecca Phillipson

Dedicated to my beautiful Mum Carrol Phillipson, thank you for everything.
Special mention to the incredibly talented Jessica Toft for the constant support.

XX

Don't judge a book by it's cover.

Contents

"For me writing a short story is a tiny window into other worlds, other minds and dreams. They are journeys that can take the reader anywhere in the universe and yet they will still be back in time for dinner."

Prologue

I'm slipping away, that's what it feels like, as if my life is slowly leaving me. I can hear screaming, lots and lots of screaming. I'm not afraid though, I'm emotionally exhausted. I need to rest now. Someone is panicking, really panicking. It's cold, ice cold, the type of cold that sends your hands blue. I can't feel my body, not properly, everything around me is really blurry, I can't really make anything out. The sounds are muffled, almost as if I'm underwater, deep below the surface. I'm consumed by darkness, trapped within the pit of it's unrelenting bleakness until a sudden, sharp light draws me in, locking my gaze. It's almost too painful to keep my eyes open. I go to shut my eyes but I am locked in it's grasp- moved harshly, jilted, shook with force. I am being held, but they need to let me go now. What happened tonight was always meant to happen and now there must be somewhere else I was always meant to be.

I didn't really do much in the eighteen years that I was alive. I had no plans, no dream careers to go after. I wasn't very good at anything, well I never tried to be. I didn't like school at all. I would avoid going in as much as I could. I left school with no qualifications whatsoever, I've never even had a job interview. I do enjoy writing though, I think if I would have gone to school and applied myself better, then I could have been good at English. Maybe I'd have gone far in that subject? But I guess it's too late now.

I was brought up in care, you see. I was left on the doorstep of a social services unit in Salford. I was left there all night and was found by a cleaner who came to work early the next day. Apparently, I had only just been born. I was left in a cardboard box with only a blanket and a photo with me. No one ever came forward for me, no one ever found out where I actually came from. I was alone in the world.

I never had a proper family, even the people that were looking after me didn't really give a shit. Family after family would take me in but never really wanted me, they probably just did it for the money. I never knew what it was like to be loved or to be wanted. I merely just existed in a world where I didn't even ask to be born. Sad really. I could only dream of a family, a nice home, a bedroom that I could relax in. Maybe a brother or a sister? Imagine that! Me- with a Mum, Dad, siblings and an actual home. I used to dream of my mum coming to find me when I was younger, taking me out of my shitty life and making it all better, but she never did, then as I got older I stopped dreaming and just accepted my shitty reality for what it was shit. The reality was, I was no one in the world and I had no one who cared.

I was eighteen when I was literally just dropped by the care system. They had done their bit and then I was on my own. I stood in the middle of a grubby bedsit in the centre of Manchester with nothing but the key in my hand, a few boxes and a debit card that the government gave me. Every month they would give me some money, not a lot, but enough to hopefully become independent. The bedsit was above a newsagents, on a busy street. Looking out of the only window there was, you could see and hear the hustle and bustle of the people living their lives. Businessmen rushing around with their laptop bags, perhaps to go back into work or to attend important meetings. Posh looking women giggling with their girlfriends heading for lunch where they would sip sweet wine and eat caviar. University students, trying to make their dreams come true away from all their family and friends. Homeless people asking for change or food. Everyone had a part to play, everyone was living their own life.

I turned around to look at my bedsit, it wasn't very big, consisting of only two rooms. A small kitchen at the back with a little table and chair, two work counters at either side, small fridge freezer, kettle, microwave and a decent washer- it had everything that I needed really. Opposite the kitchen was a single bed to the left and a wardrobe to the right, slightly blocking a sliding door into a small bathroom. It did have a bath though, so that was a bonus. I walked over to it and I caught my reflection in the grubby, dirty bathroom mirror. I wiped the mirror with my sleeve and stood observing myself. My naturally brown, wavy hair, down, just past my shoulders. My pale face and red cheeks looked tired. My green, worn hoodie that I'd had for years over my black ripped jeans and white trainers. I wasn't much, but I was real. I suddenly felt myself smile. I was nobody in the world, no one ever wanted me. I didn't even know who I was to be honest, but there I was, alive and well. I thought about what I wanted and needed the most in the world. It was the same thing I had always wanted. It was the first thing I thought about when I woke up and the last thing I thought about at night- the truth. Where the hell did I come from? What was my story? I didn't have a lot of money, I didn't have a lot of time, but I was determined to find out.

The day she discovered the truth, was the day I died. I waited my whole life for that one moment, and in a flash it was all over. I remember how it felt, that feeling when you know you're never going to wake up again. When you can feel yourself drifting off. But I'll tell you more about that later.

My name is Zoe, just Zoe. The name is actually of Greek Origin and comes from the name Eve, which ironically means life- eternal life. What I am about to tell you is my unbelievable truth. It's true what they say you know...

life really does flash before your very eyes.

Chapter 1
The Beginning

    I didn't have many belongings, Christmas and birthdays were never special when moving from one family to the next, most of the gifts I got were edible or plastic. Nothing ever lasted or really felt like mine. I only had two boxes to unpack, mainly clothing. I did have a canvas of a young girl that I found one day in someone's yard. They were throwing it away because some of the paint had smudged, but I liked it, so I took it. The young girl was at the fair, sat on a white carousel horse, watched by her family nearby. She was wearing a bright red coat and the rest of the painting was black and white. I couldn't take my eyes off it, in some ways imagining me as that little girl caught in a moment of happiness surrounded by her family.

    I took the canvas and placed it on the wall above my bed where I found a small hook that was half hanging out. I also had a small tin box that I had for as long as I could remember. I sat on my bed with it and opened it, inside was a picture of my mum, the picture was old, worn, ripped around the edges. I had it since I was a baby and it's always been kept with me. My mum looked very young, younger than I was at that time. So, in my head I knew that's probably why she wouldn't really want me. Her hair was long and brown, she had pale skin too. She must have been at home when the picture was taken because she was laying on some grass, sunbathing, smiling cheekily at the camera, as if whoever took the picture caught her by surprise. On the back of it someone had written *'I hope you live a happy life'* in pencil and it felt rushed because I could only just make out what it said. I figured Mum must have written on the back of it before she let some total strangers take me away. That was it, that's all I had of my past. That's all I had to go on in the world. It wasn't much was it?

It was still light out, summer was approaching so I decided to go and explore Manchester. I was brought up on the outskirts and had never actually been into the city centre before. I suddenly had a new lease of life, a purpose. It felt great. I was literally in the heart of where everything was going on, bars, clubs, restaurants, museums, shopping centres, so it didn't take me long until I found a quirky looking bar to sit outside off, it was called The Plant Pot and the entire building was covered in wild looking flowers. I didn't have much money, only the support from the government but I had never done anything like that before, so I decided to splash out a little and treat myself. I ordered a beer and sat outside, observing the people around me. I kept thinking about my mum. What if she was famous? Maybe an Actress or something? What if she was one of those posh women who drank champagne for dinner? A rush of excitement raced through my body, as I started to feel alive, I started to feel what living was really like. But where did I start? I didn't even know if my mum still lived in Manchester, she could be anywhere in the world. But I had to try, didn't I? I had nothing to lose. Nothing at all.

A few days later I was sat at my table in my bedsit staring at the photo of my mum. Flicking the edges of the picture and staring at the canvas of the girl on the carousel horse, I thought hard about what to do. What could I do today that could help me start this process? Then it clicked, I'll go back to where it all started, where my life began, alone and cold on the step of the social services offices in Salford. I grabbed my phone, keys and headed for the tram. I was on the tram for ages, stopping at every stop. I was impatient, I just wanted to get there and start asking questions. The offices were on a large industrial estate far away from civilization.

I was told about my shitty start in life by Elaine- A stuck up social worker who really couldn't be bothered with her job. Elaine told me when I was old enough to understand, maybe fourteen, what had happened to me. I was always asking questions. I think I annoyed the social workers because they just started ignoring me. I remember Elaine the most, she used to walk up to me, her designer handbag hanging off her arm.
"Come here Zoe, quickly, I don't have long." Her hair was bleach blonde and curled to perfection, she wore false

eyelashes that looked like huge spiders, and her lips were the brightest red I had ever seen. She always smelt of strong perfume, it always made me sneeze which made her look at me like I was some horrible disease. I didn't really like her. I just used to feel like an inconvenience, just something she had to tick off her work schedule. Less than 5 minutes it took her to tell me everything that was known about me.

"So, you were left in a box not long after you had been born. We have no birth certificate for you, no one ever came forward to claim you. You were found by the cleaner who had come to start her shift, she brought you in and called the police. Then you ended up here, happy days." she said, rushing through her bullet point list. I never ever forgot Elaine, for all the wrong reasons.

The tram stopped. I looked out of the muggy window and saw Salford station. I clasped my hands and rushed off the tram. I got out my phone and entered the postcode for the industrial estate where the offices were, it was a thirty minute walk away. I followed where my phone was telling me to go, looking around at the place where my life started. I walked past blocks and blocks of flats. Did my mum live somewhere like that? Maybe she couldn't afford to have me? Maybe she had no choice? So many questions racing in my head.

I walked past some nicer looking houses with: gardens, plants, trees. Maybe she lived somewhere like that? Maybe I didn't fit in with her plans? Maybe she wanted more than a stupid baby? I got closer and closer, then without warning, I was there.

The surroundings were very ghetto, lots of broken beer bottles, unfinished work, not a safe space to leave a baby. Maybe it was nicer back then? I tried so hard to justify it in my head. I walked up the muddy drive to a blue door, in small writing on a grey plaque it said Social Services Unit 1. I looked down at the cracked step leading up into the unit, the place where I was left. I could not believe that anyone could leave their baby in such a horrible place. I shook my head in disbelief and rang the buzzer underneath the sign, no one answered so I rang it again.

"It's open!" a female voice yelled. I pushed the heavy, blue door and found myself standing in a cold, grey bunker. There were some plastic white chairs around the edge of the room, a few tables covered in leaflets, some had blown onto the floor and a reception desk in the centre. There were no windows, just really bad yellow lighting, that flickered at random moments. I walked up to the receptionist desk. There was no one there.

"Hello?" I said, a little unsure of what I was even going to say next. All of a sudden a woman rushed out and sat down behind the desk. She was old looking, maybe late fifties, black hair, tied in a bun on top of her head, heavy makeup, her arms were covered in tattoos.

"Sorry, yes, what do you want?"

"I want to talk to someone about something." I said quietly.

"Okay, about what?"

"Erm, me I guess."

"Oh love, don't you have some friends or something that you would be better off speaking too? I really don't have time for this." the woman said almost ushering me out of sight with her can't be bothered attitude.

"No. I need to speak to you about something that happened here eighteen years ago." I replied.

"Bloody hell, I only started this job a few months ago, so I can't help you."

"I was left here, outside, on the doorstep when I was a baby. I'm trying to find out who I am." I said with desperation.

"Love, that's shit, yeah. Life is shit. But look at you, you're alive, pretty. If someone left their baby out there in that shit hole, then they don't deserve you kiddo. Seriously go live your life."

I could feel myself getting frustrated, even then, no one cared to help me, but I wasn't about to give up.

"Can I leave you my number? Maybe you'll remember something or could ask anyone else that works here, if they know about a baby being left? Please?"

"Yes, fine, okay." I wrote my name and number on the back of a piece of paper and gave it to the woman who looked at what I had read. I smiled at her before heading for the door.

"Zoe." The woman shouted after me.

"The only person you can rely on in this world is yourself."
I nodded and left. It was freezing outside, it had also
started to rain, not the greatest start to finding out the
truth. I couldn't wait to get home. Wow, I said it. I couldn't
wait to get home, to my safe space, my happy place away
from everyone and everything. I didn't even realise it but I
did, didn't I? I had a home.

A few days later, I was wandering around the
shopping centre, looking for some home furnishings. I had
just been paid from the government so I had a little to
spare. I went to the Bargain Bucket shop to look for a few
things to brighten up my bedsit. I quite enjoyed it. I started
to find enjoyment in things that I thought I would never do,
because 'what would be the point?' was always my
attitude. There was no one to share anything with anyway
I always used to tell myself, but everything started to
change. At that moment I wasn't doing it for anyone else,
but for me. I browsed the shelves to see what I could find.
It was really busy with families trying to get all the
bargains, kids pushing things off the shelves and playing
with things they shouldn't be, but I didn't mind. After about
half an hour I decided on three small artificial plants, a
bright red clock and a vase in the shape of a love heart.
On my way back home, I even stopped off at the local
shop and picked a bunch of fresh flowers, the yellowest
sunflowers caught my eye. I only spent around £10.00 in
total, but a rush of excitement rushed through me as I
walked back to my pad.

I put the artificial plants in the window, the clock next to my canvas and the flowers and vase at the centre of my table. I took a step back and smiled at myself, slowly things were looking up. I was becoming proud of what I had started to achieve, it might have only been small changes, but it was a start, and a good one. That night I went back to The Plant Pot pub, it was very busy, I had to stand for a while until a seat became free at the bar. I sat down, looking at everyone with their friends and families having a nice time. I thought how nice it would be one day to maybe have someone to drink with, to talk to, to share things with. My world was lonely but I was used to it and at that time, a little bit okay about it.

"You want another drink love?" the barman said.

"Yeah, go on then, beer please." I tapped my card as my phone started ringing. I struggled to get it out of my pocket.

"Sorry, thanks." I said, rushing to the barman.

"Hello."

It was silent.

"Hello." I repeated.

"Hi, is that Zoe?"

"Who is this?" I asked, a little confused.

"You are Zoe, aren't you?"

"I think you have the wrong number."

"I know what happened to you. I know what happened to you as a baby."

I couldn't believe what I was hearing. My hands started to shake. I couldn't get any words out.

"Are you still there Zoe?"

"Yes, yes, still here."

"I saw you leave the social unit the other day, you left your number with Andrea didn't you?"

"Andrea? Oh right, yeah. What do you know about me?"

"Not over the phone. Can I see you? Meet you somewhere?"

I didn't know what I was supposed to say, but I needed answers, this is what I wanted, this was what I was fighting for- the truth.

"Alright, there's a pub called The Plant Pot? You know it?"

"Yes I think so, shall I meet you tomorrow, about 1.30pm?"

"Yep."

"Bye Zoe."

The phone call ended. I sat at the bar staring into my beer. That was it, the start of the journey. I could not believe how quick it had happened, it certainly felt too good to be true. What if she's a con? What if she's not? What if she tells me horrible things about my mum? What if she tells me my family are all dead and I really am alone? I couldn't stop, my head racing with all these thoughts and ideas. I drank my drink and left. That night I did not sleep at all.

It was 5.30am, on a cold, wet Wednesday morning in Manchester. The morning after the phone call from the woman who told me she could tell me about what happened. I was on edge to say the least. I felt sick to my stomach every time I thought about meeting her. Maybe I was better off not knowing? Maybe the truth was worse than I ever expected? It was a very long morning waiting with anticipation, but eventually it got to 1.30pm. I made my way nervously to the pub, where we had arranged to meet. When I walked in, it wasn't very busy, just a couple, sitting at the bar. The people who worked there had started to recognise me by that point, it became my local, which was nice to say.

"Beer love?" The bartender said, I didn't know his name yet. I nodded. Whilst I was waiting for my drink, I could feel someone staring at me from the table in the window. I glanced over, a woman was sitting there, she did not look away. We locked eyes – she was old and frail looking, had blonde hair just hanging down cascading over a big brown winter coat that looked like a big bear. After a few minutes she smiled at me and nodded. My heart sank, that was her, the woman who knew, who had all the answers, she was right there, in front of me. I approached her slowly.

"Sit down. It's alright." she said, reassuring me. The woman kept staring at me. I looked down to the floor, not really knowing what to say.

"Is that really you?" she said. I looked up at her, my eyes started to water.

"You really are a beautiful young lady." she said, wiping a tear from her eye.

"You said you could help me?" I asked, longing for answers. The woman moved closer to the table, I did the same. She paused for a while.

"I remember that morning as if it were yesterday, such a cold morning, freezing in fact. I had forgotten my gloves and I remember rubbing my hands together trying to keep them warm. I used to walk to work, I never had a car or anything luxurious like that. I'd go every morning, 4am until 8am, cleaning the social units and car park. I had to walk an hour for that job, the pay was crap but I had a family, you do what you have to. I was always tired at that time, not really with it. When I got outside the unit there was a car with it's headlights on full beam, a black car I think. It was odd because I was always the only one on site until 8ish, when the odd delivery person would come and go. I looked over at the car but there wasn't anyone in it. The back door had been left wide open. I went to have a closer look when this woman rushed back to the car, she was crying, hysterical she was, she fell into me. I asked if she was alright, but she didn't say anything, she just shut the car door and drove off at speed.

"Hang on a minute, woman?"
"Yes, mid thirties, maybe older."
"That doesn't make any sense. I have this photo that was left with me. It's of a young blonde girl, younger than me, laid on some grass, smiling at the camera."

"I never saw a photo."

"On the back of it, it said *'I hope you live a happy life'*."

"I never saw a photo Hun, maybe she hid it in your clothes. I honestly don't know. It all happened so fast, I was scared to be honest. I mean, she could have been anyone, no one would hear me scream up there, alone. Anyway, I walked to let myself in and I could hear crying, baby crying. I thought I was going mad. There was a box, a cardboard box on the step. I hesitated at first, thinking it was all a set up, someone playing a prank. But there you were, this beautiful baby girl, looking back at me. I froze. I didn't know what to do. I ran back to see if the woman was anywhere nearby but she was long gone. I rushed back to you and held you in my arms. I took you inside and wrapped you in my coat before ringing the police. When the police got there, they took a statement and that was it, they said that they would look after you. I never saw you again. I tried to ask about you on my cleaning shifts, but I was just the cleaner, a-nobody, everyone went back to pretending like I didn't exist. The woman stopped talking and took a large mouthful of her drink before looking up at me.

My eyes were full of tears, imagining what this woman had told me, I mean that actually happened, that was me.

"You said the woman, my mum, was crying?"

"Yes, the most upset I had ever seen anyone."

"So maybe my mum didn't really want to leave me? Maybe there was a reason for all this and it will all eventually make sense?" I asked, trying to reassure myself that surely if she was crying then she did want and love me. The woman looked at me with sympathy, holding out her hand for mine. I put my hand on the table and she held it tight.

"There is something else." she said, unsure of whether to tell me or not.

"I don't know if it will lead you to anything or if it's even hers but if you want to know who you are, then who am I to stop you."

I watched as the woman reached into her pocket and pulled out a small white card.

"This was left in the middle of the road." she said, handing it to me. It was a business card for a hair salon in Manchester, Hair and Beauty by Vanessa.

"Why didn't you go to the police with this?" I was a little frustrated, they could have tracked her down, my life could have been so different.

"Look Zoe, I rang the police and made sure you were safe. I didn't want to get involved any further. I had my own family to worry about, it might not even be hers anyway." I nodded and stood up from the table. I didn't drink any of my beer. I turned around to the woman before I left.

"What's your name?"

"Sandra, my name is Sandra." I smiled slightly.

"Thank you Sandra." I left the pub and walked home.

When I got back, I sat on my bed staring at the card she had given me. Was this my mum's salon? Does she still work there? Who is the girl in the photo? Maybe my sister? Everything was getting more complicated instead of clearer. I turned onto my side holding onto the card as if it was the most precious thing in the world, who knew, maybe it was.

Chapter 2
Hair And Beauty By Vanessa

The streets were quiet, very quiet, not many people about, not much traffic either. It was 6am, Friday morning. A few days after meeting Sandra for the first time. I wasn't sure what to do with what she told me, with what she gave me. I guess even though I had no idea what I was doing, I had to see this through. I needed to keep going and get to the truth, however bad it might be. I deserved that, I deserved to know. I made my way down some alleyways that lead to a much nicer part of the city. I walked through a well lit, well kept park area and when I got to the other side, there it was! Right in front of me, just like google maps had shown me, polished to perfection, painted black and gold, there it was Hair and Beauty by Vanessa.

I stood for a few minutes, taking in everything I could see. Then I walked a little closer, big portraits hung in the windows of the most beautiful looking girls with the most amazing hairstyles. There were luxury hair products in display units, some of them were £100's of pounds. How does anyone afford them? I thought. I pressed my hand against the window trying to see more, inside looked just as glamorous, everything gold and black, very glittery and shiny. Nothing out of place, it must have been one of the best salons in Manchester. I looked at the opening times, stencilled on the door, it opened at 9am. I decided to go back to the park and wait. I wasn't sure what my plan was but I was sure if I sat there for long enough, I would eventually figure it out.

It started getting busier, more cars on the road and more people on their way to work, on their way to start their day. It got to around 8.45am and I saw a young girl walk to the front of the salon, she was very stylish. Blonde hair cut in the most perfect bob, her makeup was just perfect too, simple but elegant. The girl wore all black clothing with a long brown overcoat, she was beautiful. I watched her unlock the salon and let herself in. What now? I started to panic, trying to think of a plan. I walked over to the salon and looked through the salon window again, as if looking for the very first time. The young girl had taken her coat off and was turning all the lights on, she noticed me through the window and smiled at me. I smiled back and it gave me a little confidence to go inside. Even though I felt very out of place in my plain, outdated clothes. I mean I had never even had a haircut at a salon before, but I decided to walk through the door with some confidence.

"Hi you alright?" I said.

"Hello babe, yeah sorry I'll be with you in a moment." I nodded and stood admiring the design of the place, the mirrors were amazing. They were huge and covered most of the walls, crystal encrusted around the edges. I had never seen anything like it in my life. The floor was jet black and lit up, it was just incredible. The young girl came back to talk to me after a few minutes, she stood behind the desk and sat down, taking a breath.

"Right, what can I do for you?"

I didn't know what to say. Should I just ask who Vanessa is? Maybe she can tell me where Vanessa was?

"Haircut." I blurted out, like an idiot.

"Can I have a haircut please?"

"We are very booked up, is it just a trim you want?"

"Yes, a trim is fine." I really could not afford it but it might have been the only way of finding out more about Vanessa.

"2pm alright for you?"

"Perfect thank you." I headed to the door.

"This is your first time with us isn't it?" the girl said.

"Yes, I just moved here."

"Well you chose the right place." the young girl laughed.

"We are the best salon in Manchester." I smiled and left the salon.

I went and got some essentials from the supermarket and headed back to my bedsit. I didn't know what to do with myself. Everything was happening so fast. I made myself some breakfast and then went for a long walk around the canal. It was only a fifteen minute walk from where I lived, and it took about an hour to walk all the way around it. I thought the walk would help me relax, but it didn't. I just kept checking my phone for the time and was totally distracted. I made my way back into the city centre and stopped off at a cafe for a sausage roll before my appointment- Good Grub- was the name- it was cheap and basic, but it was fine.

A young couple caught my eye, maybe in their twenties, they looked very young. The woman was breastfeeding her baby and the young man was colouring with a maybe two year old boy sitting on his knee. They must have just finished eating because there was food all over the table and floor. They were wearing joggers, their clothes had marks on, food, stains, they looked worse than I did in my hoodie. They all had a scruffy appearance, not well groomed. I wasn't one to judge, I didn't look much better. But I noticed how close they all looked, the little boy was laughing his head off, giggling away, the dad telling him how much he loved him. It was nice to see, they clearly didn't have much but I could tell how much those parents loved those kids. I was sad that it wasn't the case for me. I was sad that it wasn't an option to keep me for my parents. It was easier to leave me in a box, on a doorstep, in the cold.

I made my way back to the hair salon, feeling anxious and scared, worried about what was going to happen, if anything at all. The salon was much busier now, people coming and going. I opened the door and the young girl from before recognised me.

"Awe take a seat Hun." I sat down nervously watching the hair stylists with their clients. Women of all ages getting their hair done, talking about their problems, drinking lattes, laughing and joking. This was definitely not my scene, but it had to be done. A few minutes later, a woman in her mid fifties came into the salon with a black cloak on, well it looked like a cloak, it was probably a very expensive coat. She had blonde shoulder length hair, it sat perfectly with a few loose curls in it, her makeup was fairly natural but you could tell that she had it on. The woman was definitely a regular in the salon, she made herself right at home, she knew everyone's name and helped herself to the coffee machine. I wished I was that glamorous looking.

"Hi love, you're my 2pm, what's your name?" I was approached by one of the hairstylists, again: young, pretty, stylish.

"Zoe." I said, a little embarrassed because of how I looked in comparison to everyone else.

"This way love." The woman ushered me to a chair at the back of the salon, she took my coat off me and gave it to the receptionist, she put a black cloak on me and showed me to my seat. All I could think about was Vanessa.

"Just a dry trim isn't it?" I nodded. I was very quiet compared to everyone else in there, they were all bubbly and loud, everyone seemed to know each other, but I tried my best.

"Do you want a coffee or anything?" the woman asked.

"No I'm alright thank you." she got her comb out and started combing through my hair. I was working up the courage to ask her what her name was, but I was terrified in case she said her name was Vanessa. What would I even say?... "oh you are Vanessa. I'm the baby you left eighteen years ago on a step..." I was panicking. I was running out of time, my hair wouldn't take that long, and I couldn't afford to keep booking in. It was now or never. "What's..." I tried to speak but there was a sudden gathering by the reception desk, loads of laughing and joking could be heard. One of the stylists rushed out with some balloons and a cake. I tried to look through the mirror to see but couldn't really make out what was going on. The woman doing my hair caught me looking in the mirror.

"It's the boss's birthday today, we're trying to keep in her good books." she laughed.

"Oh right."

"You worked here long?" I felt like the conversation was natural. I felt a little more at ease to engage.

"Yes, almost ten years."

"Wow, that's a long time."

"Happy Birthday!!" Everyone shouted, the salon door burst open and everyone started singing, the clients were all engaging too, everyone was clapping and getting involved, everyone but me. I couldn't wait to leave, it was all very full on.

"Happy Birthday Vanessa!" I heard one of the clients shout across the salon. I couldn't believe it. I almost fell off my chair. Did they just say Vanessa?! I still couldn't see anyone, it was too crowded.

"Thank you my darling, thank you everyone." I heard from the crowd. Before I knew it, the woman was asking me if my hair was alright. She had finished all ready.

"Erm, yeah, sorry."

"No worries, your hair is in really good condition, it feels beautiful."

"Thank you."

"I'm Emily by the way, hope to see you again."

"Yeah, you too Emily." I took off the cloak and headed to the receptionist desk to pay and to get my coat. I waited to one side, with people still gathering around, chatting, some of the clients were standing up with foils and rollers in their hair. I didn't know where to put myself.

"Right, who's got the champagne? It is my birthday after all." a voice said in the distance. Just as the receptionist was approaching me, a woman appeared from the hustle and bustle of people, making her way to a bottle of champagne that was sitting on the reception desk with silver, glittery glasses. I paused, unable to move, my gosh… there she was. Everything seemed to slow down around me, everyone else disappeared, it felt like it was just me and her. This woman was beautiful, like something out of a magazine. She had dark blonde hair, a little bit longer than a bob. Her hair looked so shiny and soft, so much volume, she had brown lipstick on, brown eyeliner, her face looked shimmery- tanned. I noticed her nails, long and painted red. She was wearing a black dress, it looked expensive, really expensive, heels to die for with black crystal zips. I couldn't take my eyes off her, was she really, was she really my mum?

All of a sudden I felt my arm being touched.

"Love your coat, it's £50.00 please."

"Thanks, what?! I mean, yes of course." I took my card out of my pocket and gave it to the young girl, "bloody expensive" I thought, but it was the least of my worries at that moment. I paid up and headed to the door to leave. On my way out Vanessa glanced at me, no reaction or anything, just a passing look. I didn't react either, I just walked out the door and headed to the park over the road.

I sat on a bench opposite the salon, watching everyone celebrate, now and again I could see Vanessa enjoying herself. What a life she had, her own salon, clearly had money, looked after herself, so why? Why didn't she want me? My life could have been so different if she had just given me a chance, a chance to see what I could do, what I could become in this world. I could have made her so proud. She had achieved so much and she didn't want me to be part of it, she didn't want me at all. I couldn't help but cry. I could have been part of that world, part of her life, I could have had opportunities, options, different career paths. Instead I was completely alone in the world with nothing. How could she do that to me, how could she?! She had given birth to me, she went through the pregnancy, if she really didn't want me then why the hell didn't she just have an abortion. She might as well have killed me!! I was losing my shit, I needed to calm down. After all, the business card might not even be related to what happened that night. I still wasn't sure of anything. But it was my only lead, so I had to try.

Forty five minutes later, Vanessa left the salon with her balloons and some gift bags.

"See you all later!" she shouted back as the door closed behind her, she started walking down the street. I didn't have a plan or anything but I decided to follow her. I followed her into the hustle and bustle of Manchester. I almost lost her at some traffic lights but I could see the balloons she was carrying so I managed to catch up with her. I followed her to a fancy bar with doormen out front. There was no way I was going to be allowed in there, not how I was dressed, so I waited over the road. I waited for hours and hours, so bored but scared if I went for a coffee or a wander around, I would miss her. Eventually Vanessa came out, she looked drunk, she had clearly been drinking a lot.

"Hold up Vanessa." A man followed her out, carrying her bags and balloons. He had pure white hair, tanned skin, wearing an expensive looking suit. He also looked like he could have been out of a magazine. Almost immediately a silver call pulled up outside and the driver helped Vanessa into the back seat. They drove off and that was it. Vanessa had gone.

That night I couldn't get Vanessa out of my head, I couldn't stop thinking about her, I became obsessed. What was she doing? What was she wearing? Who were her friends? Her family? I wanted to know more, I wanted to know everything.

Chapter 3
First Interaction

    The next day I was back in the park watching the salon. The same girl as before opened up, but no sign of Vanessa. I was about to give up when I noticed the same silver car from the night before, it was pulling up outside the salon. I watched with anticipation, the driver got out of the car and went over to open the door at the back- it was her. Vanessa stepped out of the car, heels first, looking like she had arrived at her movie premier. Her hair was down with loose curls, she had a green trouser suit on with a big white fur coat, her oversized bag hanging off her arm- obviously designer. It had some big writing across it but I couldn't quite make it out. She was wearing the biggest, black sunglasses on her head, it wasn't even sunny, but she owned it, she looked fabulous. She went into the salon and started fussing around the reception desk, I could see her through the window, the car drove off and she disappeared for a bit. I went and grabbed a takeaway coffee from a pop up shack in the park and sat on the bench with it.

    Half an hour later, she left, so I binned my coffee cup and followed her again, this time she went into a place called The Latte House. I stood outside for ages, but she never came out, so this time I went in. It was very nice inside- posh, obviously. I expected nothing else, but it did feel a little bit more relaxed. Everything was a different shade of brown, tables and chairs dotted around the place, some lounge areas with footstools. It wasn't very busy, a woman with some shopping bags in the window, a middle aged couple reading the newspaper, some girlfriends having a spot of lunch. I scanned the room and saw Vanessa sat in the corner, scrolling on her phone. I walked over to the counter, and a young man approached me.

"Latte please." I said.

"I'll bring it over." I nodded and thought about where to sit. I sat on a table that was about three tables away from Vanessa, but I sat on the chair facing her. I took my phone out of my pocket, then put it back in again, then nearly dropped it, then left it on the table in a panic. The guy brought me my drink and I stared at it, hoping I would figure out what the hell to do next. I felt sick, my hands went clammy, I was fidgeting, I know I was, I couldn't sit still. Then I saw Vanessa look up at me, I didn't know what to do so I just smiled, she gave half a smile back and started drinking her coffee, still scrolling through her phone. I felt like I was going to pass out, I became hot, really hot, burning in fact. I got up from where I was and ran to the toilets at the back of the coffee shop. As soon as I got to the toilets, I threw up. I couldn't control myself. I don't think I had thought about just how serious this was. Maybe I wasn't ready to know what happened to me? But

I felt like I had nothing else in the world going for me, finding out the truth gave me purpose, it gave me a reason to get up. Moments later I heard the door open, then I felt my cubicle door being pushed so I quickly pushed it too and locked it.

"You alright in there." I heard. Shit, I think it was Vanessa, her voice sounded posh, very posh, she must have followed me in.

"Yeah."

"Come out."

"I'm alright."

"Don't worry, I'll wait." I had nowhere to go, and she wasn't leaving. I got up and opened the door. Vanessa stood in front of me, leaning on the sink, with her arms folded. She stared at me for what felt like minutes before reaching for some paper towels. She walked over to me and put one of her hands under my chin, before wiping my eyes with the towels.

"Do I know you?" she asked.

"I've been in your salon."

"That will be it then, you have the most beautiful hair, is it natural?" she said, whilst finishing wiping my eyes. I nodded. Vanessa threw the paper towels in the bin, checked herself in the mirror and then headed for the door.

"My daughter has naturally wavy hair. You look after yourself, make sure you eat properly, you don't half look pale." Then she left.

What just happened? Like seriously? She had a daughter? What? Did she just say she had a daughter? But how? Why? I couldn't get my head around it, when I left the toilets she had gone. Have we got this wrong? Maybe Vanessa has nothing to do with me after all? Maybe the card that Sandra found was just there by mistake? Maybe Vanessa wasn't the woman that left me all those years ago. I was so bloody confused.

    The next day I was sitting in The Plant Pot Pub waiting for Sandra, I had just ordered a beer.
"There you go trouble." The Barman said, placing my beer in front of me, wiping a table next to ours. I couldn't help but smile. I had never really paid any notice to him before, I had always been somewhere else in my head but he was nice, really nice. He had kind green eyes, black curly hair, beard, and lots of tattoos. He looked strong, the kind of guy that would protect you. He was just nice. Sandra soon came rushing in, she sat down eager to know what had happened.
"She's fucking loaded, she owns that salon you know, she drinks champagne and calls everyone darling." I said, sarcastically.
"She did alright for herself then."
"Understatement, she's glamorous, like really glamorous, dressed head to toe in designer stuff."
"Must be nice."
"I met her! I spoke to her Sandra."

"What? Where?"

"I've been following her, she was in this coffee shop. I ended up running to the bathroom to throw up and she followed me in, she started saying how beautiful my hair was and then she said... my daughter's got naturally wavy hair." I said, trying to mimic Vanessa's voice.

"Hang on a minute, she said that."

"Yeah, she has a daughter."

I paused for a moment. I knew what I was about to say might not go down well.

"I need you to do something for me." Sandra looked apprehensive.

"I need you to go to the salon."

"No. No. Absolutely not." Sandra sat back in her chair, folding her arms, looking stubborn.

"Please. I need to know if it's her you saw that night or if I'm just wasting my time. Please. Help me." I waited for to respond, she sat forward, leaning onto the table, putting her head in her arms.

"Fine, alright, yes." I sighed with relief.

"That's on the house by the way." The Barman said, smiling over at me, he was wiping a table next to ours.

"Oh yeah and what you called handsome." Sandra teased.

"Jack." he grinned.

"Well Jack, I'm Sandra and this is Zoe." I was so embarrassed. Jack winked at me and went to serve some other customers.

"He likes you!" Sandra joked. I wasn't really in the mood to start flirting with anyone. Jack was lovely and he did make me smile but I had bigger things to worry about.

Sandra and I stood like rabbits in the headlights opposite the salon.
"Bloody hell." Sandra said, admiring it for the first time.
"There, there!." I grabbed hold of Sandra's arm and pointed to the salon.
"Where?"
"Stood in the window, on the phone! That's her."
"Right." Sandra rushed over the road and into the salon. I shouted after her but she wouldn't come back.
"Sandra!! Shit." She was in there for ages. I was getting worried. What is she doing? What is she saying? Shall I go in? I was pacing, messing about with my hands, almost itching the skin off them. Eventually I saw Sandra rushing out.
"Thank you, have a nice day." She said, the door closing behind her.
"What did you say? Was it her? Was it?" I wanted to know everything. Sandra didn't say anything, she just walked in front of me, expecting me to follow, which of course I did. Where did we end up? The Plant Pot... If it wasn't my local before it definitely was that day.
We both rushed in flustered. Jack noticed us straight away, his eyes lit up.
"Twice in one day."

"Beer and large red." Sandra said, rushing for a seat.

"Well?" I followed her, more than eager. I waited and waited and waited.

"It's her." I could feel my eyes getting bigger.

"You sure?"

"There's a certain type of class you never forget, like you're almost apologising for being in their presence. It's her, Vanessa is the woman I saw that night, she's the woman who left you."

I sat there and just sobbed. Why didn't she want me? She had a daughter? So why didn't she want me too? Sandra reached for my hands across the table and held them tight. I had never had that before, for the first time, I felt like someone actually gave a shit about me.

"You're sure?" My voice was small. Sandra nodded.

"She looks the same as she did all those years ago, that will be the Botox mind." Sandra said, trying to lighten the conversation.

"Okay, thank you." I was ready to go home, I had enough.

"Give me half an hour." Sandra said, rushing up from the table.

"What? Where are you going?"

"Don't move." Sandra drank her wine in one mouthful and left. Not long after Jack came over with a tissue.

"Anything you want to talk about?" he said, softly. I shook my head. He put his hand on my shoulder and cleared some tables. I just couldn't get my head around any of it. None of it made sense.

Before I knew it Sandra was back. She sat down with purpose and ordered us some more drinks and waited for Jack to bring them over before she spoke.

"How do you get people like Vanessa to notice you?" Sandra said, waiting for me to respond. I just glared at her, thinking what on earth is this woman going on about. "You become her." she said, looking more than impressed with herself.
"What are you talking about?"
"You need to transform yourself, Zoe. You need to look the part, act the part. You need a job, money. You need to be part of her world."
"Have you lost your mind?" I said, sitting back in my chair, laughing, convinced Sandra had lost the plot.
"You are going to become like Vanessa. And I'm going to help you."

Sandra reached into her bag and placed a large white envelope in front of me. I looked at her hesitantly before reaching for the envelope- it was heavy. When I looked inside I could not believe my eyes. It was money, lots and lots of money. I had never seen that much money before. I was overwhelmed.
"Where did you get all that?" I whispered.
"My life savings. I'm giving it to you."
"You can't! You have a family."

"I did have a family, it didn't work out. I have a son Zack but he's living some high class life in London, he doesn't bother."

"Why are you doing this for me?"

"What you said to me when we first met. Maybe your life could have been different if I would have given the card to the police. Maybe I could have done more for you. Life's too short Zoe. Please, let me help you." I took a moment tapping my fingers on the table. Eventually I nodded, tears falling down my face.

"Thank you." I said, barely able to get the words out.

"Right girl, we have some serious shopping to do." Sandra lifted her glass to me.

"Here's to finding out the truth."

I know what you're thinking. I thought the same. It's hard to believe how fast everything was happening. Within months I had gone from a young eighteen year old girl, dropped from the care system and not really knowing my place or purpose in society, to a girl with a plan. A home of sorts, and now this woman Sandra, who was like this guardian angel. I didn't know her at all, I mean, she could have been anyone but somehow, I felt safe. I did trust her and even just being in her presence made me feel warm. I thought her idea was insane and I never thought it would work but like I keep saying, I didn't have anything to lose. I think timing is important, the idea that everything happens for a reason. It's what we turn to when something doesn't quite work out, or if something bad happens. But with my situation, I really do believe that every single thing that happened after Sandra gave me that money was always meant to be. Even the bad things, the ugly things, the most unimaginable things. Sometimes you just have to live the hand you've been dealt.

Chapter 4
Material Girl

A few days later, Sandra and I met to go shopping. I was nervous but also a tiny bit excited. I could only dream of doing things like what I was about to do. We stood looking up at the most luxurious, designer brand boutiques in Manchester called Marilyn's, we were both speechless. The building itself was immaculate, mannequins stood in the mirrors wearing the most glamorous looking outfits. There was a red carpet at the entrance with hanging baskets of fresh flowers above. I couldn't believe we were actually going inside.

"How much do we have to spend?" I asked, like an excited kid standing at the gates to Disneyland.

"Around £15,000." Sandra said, opening the door.

"How much?!" I nearly fell over my feet. That was so much money!

When we walked through the spiral door, things only got better. Everything was a deep red colour, very bold. Designer clothing hung on silver rails all around the store, glass tables dotted around, displaying bags, shoes, belts and accessories in the most beautiful way. I could see the changing rooms to the back of the shop, heavy looking red curtains with gold detail hanging around oval shape mirrors and more chaise lounges. A woman who worked there made her way over to us, she was done up to perfection- of course she was. Dark hair tied back in a neat bun, black dress, black shoes, lots of makeup.

"Can I help you?" she asked, almost condescending.

"We would like to try everything." Sandra said, getting excited. The woman who's name badge said 'Carla' looked us both up and down, clearly judging us. It was a horrible feeling you know.

"Some of these items are hundreds, even thousands of pounds." Carla said, with a monotone voice. Sandra nodded and walked over to me. She reached for the white envelope and started flicking through the notes.

"I suppose we could always spend this money somewhere else." Carla's eyes lit up when she saw the money and her approach instantly changed towards us.

"I'm so sorry Madam, let me get you both something to drink and I'll put some things to one side for you. Feel free to have a browse." Carla rushed off to the back of the store.

"Stick with me kiddo." Sandra laughed, making her way around the clothes. I didn't know where to start, everything was just mesmerising to me. Moments later Carla came back with two glasses of champagne.

"There you go ladies. I've put some items over in the dressing rooms for you, let me know if you need any help." Sandra nodded, taking the champagne off the silver tray and handing me one. We then made our way to the dressing rooms and sat down on one of the chaise lounges. I walked over to the clothes rail of all the designer clothes, I touched them with my hand, they felt amazing, like silk, so soft. I pulled the red curtain around me and started trying all the clothing on. I remember how they felt in comparison to my usual clothes, just unreal. The first thing I tried on was a white top with the words 'Marilyn' written all over it in black. I matched it with some black skinny jeans. I looked in the mirror and couldn't believe what a difference an outfit could make. I started to feel more confident the more I tried. Sandra was there each time, waiting to see what I had on to give me the thumbs up. I spent hours trying all kinds of clothing on- tops- jumpers-jeans-trousers- anything you could think of, I tried it.

"Carla, have you got anything red?" I heard Sandra say whilst I was getting myself into another outfit.

"No...Actually yes! Hang on." I pulled back the curtain in a green jumpsuit to see what Carla was bringing back.

"This is from a few seasons ago, it's been in the back for years." Carla stood holding the most magical looking red fishtail dress, with turtle neck top. It was backless with crystals around the fishtail area. Carla brought it to me and closed the curtain around us. I watched through the mirror as Carla helped me get into the beautiful dress. I couldn't believe how amazing I looked. Was that really me?

"Wow." I heard Carla say, as she finished ruffling up the fishtail part of the dress, she stood behind me and smiled at me through the mirror. Carla slowly pulled back the red curtain and I turned to face Sandra. I could feel my eyes start to go as I looked up to Sandra, her face dropped, her eyes went red, she walked over to me and took hold of my hands.

"You're beautiful Zoe, so beautiful." she wrapped her arms around me. No one had ever hugged me before, no one. I felt loved, I felt wanted, I felt like I had someone in my shitty world to share things with. Sandra was like a proud mother in that moment, and it was the best feeling ever.

We left that boutique, having spent thousands and thousands of pounds, carrying bag after bag of designer clothing. We made our way around some other designer shops and luxury brand boutiques. I stocked up on underwear, all matching sets, floral designs and pretty colours. I had never had matching underwear before, so I was excited to start. I also stocked up on a range of accessories and sunglasses. I even had my makeup professionally done in a cosmetic store. I felt like royalty, sat in a chair whilst everyone was fussing around me. I had never even worn makeup before, the lady said I had really good skin (yeah I even started calling people lady), she applied some light foundation to my skin, with bronzer and highlighter, a little mascara and a nude lip. When she held up the mirror, again I was shocked. I was starting to look like 'those types' of girls I admired growing up. I bought all the makeup I needed and then we headed to lunch.

I took Sandra to the greasy spoon cafe Good Grub, where I saw that young family. We sat down at one of the tables.

"You know we can go anywhere you want?" Sandra said, looking around at the cluttered tables and chairs.

"I like it here." Sandra sat down and we waited, surrounded by our bags, for the women who worked there to give us our menus. We ordered fish, chips and peas, with two teas. I don't know why I liked that cafe so much, I guess it just felt real.

"Just one more thing to do now." Sandra said, folding some fish into some bread.

"What?" I asked with a mouthful of food.

"Your hair! It's time to be a blonde." she said, taking a big bite of her sandwich, giving me a smile. She could tell that I was unsure.

"Trust me, alright?" I nodded. I did trust Sandra, I really did. I couldn't imagine my life without her anymore. I felt safe with her, knowing I had her there was so comforting.

After dinner we made our way over to a hairdressers in the shopping centre Unique Forever, it wasn't as fancy as Vanessa's but it was still nice. Everything matched and complemented each other, white and grey colour scheme. It was neat and tidy with just a few small display units of the products they were selling. I must have sat in that bloody salon chair for hours and hours, watching as the hairdresser bleached my entire head. Sandra was sitting at the back, reading the free magazines and enjoying the free coffee. I was getting bored, I couldn't wait for it to be over. Once the bleach had been washed off, the hairdresser asked how much I wanted cut off, Sandra got up like a shot.

"A bob, cut a bob, longer at the front." I didn't even get the chance to speak. I looked at Sandra in the mirror and she winked at me. I watched as my hair was snipped away. I was worried, I won't lie. A bob was a massive change, but as she started drying my hair it all really came together. It wasn't bleach blonde, it was more like an ash blonde. I didn't even look like me, especially with my makeup that I had done before, I looked hot. Sandra came and stood next to the hairdresser who was finishing off with some hair products.

"Yep, I think we are good to go." Sandra was so excited.

Sometimes I think she wanted to find out the truth as much, maybe even more than I did. After we had finished at the salon, it was getting late so Sandra got the bus back and I made my way to my bedsit, with my hundreds of shopping bags. When I got home I crashed out on the bed, all my shopping bags dropped around me. I was exhausted and all I wanted to do was sleep. What a day though, bye bye Zoe, hello new me!

I had worked on my look, now I needed a job. I remember the first time I went out as the *'new me'*- it was

44

overwhelming. I wore black jeans, black boots, a white oversized jumper and a denim jacket, with a small black handbag. My hair was neat and I wore a little makeup. Everyone noticed me, people actually acknowledged me in the street, people would say "*morning*" and "*hello*", they would smile at me as we passed each other. I was starting to fit into society. People assumed I was someone in the world, they assumed I had a job, money, I had a good life. Is that all it took to get noticed? A nice outfit and fresh hair-do? Is the world really that shallow?

When I walked into the pub later on, Jack didn't even recognise me at first.
"Oh my god. Zoe is that you?" He was in shock.
"Yes Jack." I said, trying to shake off the attention he was giving me.
"You look fit! Sorry... good, you look good." Jack was getting flustered, he went red. I appreciated he thought I looked nice, but I still didn't think I needed fussing over.
"I'll bring you a drink over." he said, trying to play it cool. I went and sat at a table and started searching for jobs on my phone. So many jobs, from Cleaners to Bartenders, Teachers to Managers of shops. You could get paid by the hour or salaried, there were things called graduate jobs and apprenticeships. There were even jobs that said they trained you. I had no idea where to start, I had absolutely no qualifications, I had nothing.

45

I clicked on one of the jobs just to be curious. It was for a job in a vets, working on the reception. The amount of qualifications you needed just to get an interview was ridiculous, it was impossible. I was exhausted, just reading through everything. Jack brought over my beer. "Thanks." I sat back in my chair, thinking about what to do, where to start. Once I'd finished my beer I headed to the newsagents and bought a selection of newspapers. I wasn't about to give up.

That afternoon and a few days to follow, I sat at my small table with stacks of newspapers in front of me. I went through every one and circled all the jobs that I was going to try and get. It was frustrating to say the least.

ZOE:
"Hi, is that Lauren?"
INTERVIEWER:
"Yes it is."
ZOE:
"I'm ringing about the job in the supermarket?"
INTERVIEWER:
"Oh yes, have you worked in a shop before?"
ZOE:
"No."
INTERVIEWER:
"How many years of customer service experience do you have?"

ZOE:
"I don't."
INTERVIEWER:
"What is your current job position?"

I hung up the phone.
Next...

ZOE:
"Hi, I'm ringing about the babysitting job advertised in the paper?"
INTERVIEWER:
"Yes, Hi. How many years have you had your DBS? Hello? Hello?"

I hung up. What the hell was a DBS?

Next...

ZOE:
"Can I speak to someone about the dog grooming job please?"
INTERVIEWER:
"Have you ever worked with animals before?
ZOE:
"Nope."
INTERVIEWER:
"I take it you're an animal lover then?"

ZOE:
"Nope. You know what, it's fine. Thanks."

Next...

ZOE:
"Is that John?"
INTERVIEWER:
"Yes. How can I help?"
ZOE:
"I'm interested in the bar job?"
INTERVIEWER:
"Have you worked in a bar before?"
ZOE:
"No."
INTERVIEWER:
"Do you have any transferable skills that you could bring to the job?"
ZOE:
"No. I don't have any transferable skills. I don't have any skills. I just need a bloody job."
I hung up the phone and threw it on the bed. This was useless I thought. I laid on my bed and just closed my eyes when my phone started ringing.

ZOE:
"Yes!" I snapped.
SANDRA:

"Bloody hell, what's wrong with you Madam?"
ZOE:
"Nothing, sorry, just one of those days."
SANDRA:
"Can you meet me in half an hour?"
ZOE:
"Yeah, I guess."
SANDRA:
"Usual place. See you soon." Sandra sounded excited, giddy.

When I got to the pub Jack wasn't there, which I was kind of pleased about, as I was starting to get worried he thought I had nothing better to do with my time. Which I suppose I didn't, but I didn't want him to know that. I waited for Sandra like she told me to, getting in our usual round of drinks. When she came in she was ecstatic, walking over to me waving her phone about in her hand.
"I think I have sorted your job situation out."
"What?" she gave her phone to me. It was a screen shot, I looked at it closer and looked back at Sandra.
"You are kidding me." It was a job advert for Vanessa's Salon, they were looking for a part time receptionist. I started reading through everything in more detail.
"Looking for someone to take bookings, greet the clients, basic admin duties, customer service is essential and experience in a similar role is desirable." I gave Sandra the phone back.

"I have no qualifications, no experience. I have nothing." I put my head in my hands. Sandra sat down and took hold of my arm.

"Listen to me. You are going to get that job. What better way to find out more about Vanessa than to become part of her world! You are not on your own, not anymore. I am not going anywhere, okay."

"There is no way I'm even going to get an interview. This is ridiculous."

"Oi come on girl, this job advertisement ends in two days, it's meant to be."

"I really don't know Sandra."

"Trust me please."

"Okay, I trust you."

"Now, drink up Madam." I watched Sandra drink her drink and I slowly drank mine.I still wasn't sure if it would actually work, but I did what Sandra said, after all, she was all I had.

Chapter 5
The Interview

We spent hours sitting at a computer in the local library that Sandra had been a member of for years. I watched closely as she made my CV.

"What's your surname?" she asked, her green glasses hanging from the end of her nose.

"Smith, it's a general one they gave because I've never had a birth certificate." Sandra looked at me and squeezed my hand. She didn't say anything. She didn't need to.

"Right, so let's say you left school with all the main GCSE's. English, maths, science. You got A's and B's. Then you left school and went straight into employment with a small family run business called Sandra's Beauty Room. That way I can give you a cracking reference. You have two years experience in admin, answering emails, phone calls and greeting and talking to clients. Do you have any hobbies?"

"No."

"Oh come on, there must be something you enjoy?"

"I like writing."

"Good, so we will highlight that." Sandra spent ages, taking bits out, putting bits in, tweaking sections. I was getting tired, I could feel my eyes going heavy staring at the white screen. Finally Sandra sat back in her chair. "And print." she said, clicking hard on the mouse. She took the piece of paper from the printer next to her and handed it to me.

"Go home, get some sleep, tomorrow is a big day." I really was so exhausted at that time. Everything was happening so fast, things were starting to come together and it was terrifying me.

It was a new day, I woke up to a message off Sandra,

SANDRA:
You can do this kiddo, Lots of love, S x

I stood in the middle of my bedsit, designer clothing hanging everywhere, my kitchen table was full of all my accessories, and shoes covered the entire floor. I had dresses hung from my window, my wardrobe was full, clothes still in bags. What the hell do I wear?! I spent about an hour searching through everything before finally deciding on what to wear. I chose a black, tight fitted dress, over the knee high mustard boots with a matching colour bag, a long, black, floral print slim coat and some big black cat eye shaped sunglasses. I straightened my hair and did my makeup as the lady in the cosmetic shop had shown me, it was natural with a nude lip. I also painted my nails black. I was ready to face the world, well, as ready as I could have been. I put my CV in my handbag and headed for the door.

On that walk to the salon, I had people wolf whistling at me, going out of their way to talk to me, people were looking at me, I mean like really looking, I felt like a celebrity. I did catch my reflection in the shop windows a couple of times and I did look amazing. I had to play the part, this was now who I was and I had a job to do. Dressed head to toe in designer gear, the salon was in sight, I took a deep breath before walking in. I didn't look around, I didn't hesitate.

"Is Vanessa in please?" I asked the girl with the blonde bob at reception, she didn't even recognise me, she almost looked star struck. I could feel everyone in there go quiet wondering who the hell I was.

"Can I take your name please?"

"Zoe. My name is Zoe."

"One moment." I stood patiently. A few moments later Vanessa came out of the back followed by the girl."

"You wanted to see me?" she said, looking me up and down.

"Hello Vanessa, I'm interested in the job you're advertising. I wanted to personally give you my resume." I handed Vanessa the piece of paper containing my fake CV, which she didn't even bother to look at.

"Is that the?" Vanessa went on to say, looking at my bag.

"Yes, it is. The new *Marilyn's* bag." she couldn't take her eyes off it. Vanessa pursed her lip up at me and started to walk away.

"Come back at 2.30pm, don't be early." she said, handing my CV to the girl with the bob. I turned around and left. I ran around the corner and screamed. I did it! I actually did it. I needed to phone Sandra.

ZOE:
"Come on! Pick up!" it was ringing for ages.
SANDRA:
"Hello?"
ZOE:
"I did it, I spoke to her! You were right, she didn't even look at my CV, she was more interested in my bloody bag! Anyway, she wants to see me at 2.30pm." I could hear Sandra coughing in the background, wheezing.
"You alright? You sound terrible."
SANDRA:
"Yeah, I just got a cold. Good girl, I knew you could do it. Speak to you later."
ZOE:
"Okay!" I was so proud of myself, I could not believe it was that easy, it all seemed too good to be true.

I still had a few hours to go before my interview so I decided to go to the cafe I liked and research interview questions and answers. When I arrived, there were quite a

54

few people in, they all looked at me. I smiled but none of them smiled back which I thought was odd.

"Tea please." I said, to the woman behind the till. I sat down and started searching on my phone. The atmosphere felt strange, it was too quiet, no one was talking. The woman brought my tea over and slammed it on the table, so much so that some of it spilled out.

"You trying to prove a point or summet?" she said, clearly angry with me.

"What?" I was confused.

"You know people come in here to feel like they belong in the world, you could go anywhere you wanted and you want to sit in here and spend 65p on a cup of tea. You should be ashamed." I couldn't believe what I was hearing. I was in so much shock at what the woman had said that I couldn't even answer her. Then I took a look around at everyone sitting in the cafe. People were sitting with ripped clothing on, marked clothes, their hair was dirty, their nails were dirty. Then I realised it was me, I was the problem. I'd walked into there wearing all designer clothes, done up to the nines and they assumed that I was mocking them.

 I realised very quickly that to belong in Vanessa's world, meant I had to leave those people behind, those real, genuine people. There was no place for me there any more. I got up and left.

"I'm sorry." I said to the woman as I left, she didn't say anything, just stood shaking her head whilst drying her hands on a grubby looking tea towel. I couldn't help but have a little cry to myself. I guess that's when I knew that this was real. What I was doing was real. There was no going back.

I arrived at my interview dead on 2.30pm still thinking about what happened at the cafe before. I was greeted by the young girl with the bob. She took me to a room at the back which was Vanessa's office. I took off my sunglasses and placed them on my head.
"Zoe's here." the girl said, before turning to me and asking if I would like a drink.
"Latte please."
"Yes, two lattes." Vanessa said not looking up at me, she was typing heavily on her laptop, then a few moments later she told me to sit down.
Her office was like the salon, covered in mirrors, black sparkly floor. Her desk was glass and abstract looking, almost like a sculpture. There were glass tables dotted around her office with awards that she had won from the salon. Behind where she was sitting was a massive window overlooking the street, it had blacked out glass so she could see out, but no one could see in. It was really nice and smelled incredible, I wasn't sure if it was her perfume or the room itself, but whatever it was, it was strong. The girl brought our lattes in and I took off my coat, placing it over my chair. Vanessa stopped typing and looked up at me. There was no small talk, no conversation

to make me feel more relaxed or comfortable, she was straight to the point.

"So, why do you think you would be good working in my salon?" she wasn't messing around. From the start she was proving that she was the one in control, she had the power, she was testing me.

"I'm strong, I'm confident, I'm dedicated, I want to achieve." I said, trying to remain calm and confident.

"This company you say you have worked for? I've never heard of them."

"They were a small, family run business."

"I think your CV is lack-less if I am honest."Vanessa said, sitting back in her throne-like chair.

"I left school with my GCSE's and went straight into paid work. I worked there for two years doing all the admin tasks. Answering emails and phone calls, greeting the clients, that's what you say you're looking for? I can do all that and I can do it well."

"I don't think you can." Vanessa said in the most smug, patronising way.

"Would it matter if I couldn't?" I replied, remaining professional.

"I beg your pardon?" Vanessa moved her latte across her desk with her hand clearing space so she could lean forward on it, arms folded, looking at me directly in the eyes.

"Let's be honest, I'm not here because of my CV. I'm here because of my bag. You know I can do this job, because you know I look the part." Vanessa was stunned at what I had said, she started studying me hard.

"You do realise this salon, my salon, is the most established salon in Manchester."

"Yes I do, I wouldn't want to work anywhere else."

I couldn't believe what was coming out of my mouth. I was absolutely fluking it but I think it sounded bloody brilliant. I had an answer for everything. I was a little bit sassy and even though I was getting nothing from Vanessa, I think underneath it all she liked me, she didn't want to but she couldn't help it. I was unapologetic, I was confident and owning myself. I was just like her. I was just like Vanessa.

"I think there are girls out there with better CVs and better clothes." she said, before ripping my CV up that was in front of her and throwing it in the bin. I laughed, put on my coat and walked to the door. Before I left I turned to face her.

"You know Vanessa, there are better salons and better owners out there too. I hope you find what you're looking for." I couldn't believe I had said that, but I did. I walked through the salon with everyone watching me. When I got to the front door it was locked, I couldn't get out. What was happening? I did not plan for this.

"Excuse me, the doors are locked." I said, a little panicked, everyone ignored me. Then I heard heels in the distance, they were getting closer to me. It was Vanessa, she stood at the top of the steps, looking down on everyone. I remember at that moment how scared I was, I didn't know what to do. I just stayed in character, trying to keep calm. "People respect me Zoe because I demand it. People want me to like them, they want me to notice them. My world is not for everyone, you know some people out there, they want to be nobodies, they don't want to be noticed but us in here, we do. My team wants to be noticed." Everyone stood silent, not daring to speak. Vanessa walked down the steps and stood right in front of me, she was intimidating and I could feel myself about to crack under the pressure.

"You got the job the minute you walked in here." she said.

Okay, I was confused. Did she just say I got the job? All of that and I got the job?

"Thank you." I said, my voice starting to shake, my cheeks going red.

"You're welcome, oh and just for the record, you never ever speak to me like that again." she said, walking away from me. Once she had left, everyone sighed with relief.

"Bloody hell, how did you manage that?" one of the hairdressers said. I couldn't speak.

"You need a drink babe, we will give you a ring at some point tomorrow." I nodded and left as quickly as I could.

Chapter 6
Friendships

I left the salon and headed to the pub, I couldn't wait to tell Sandra the news. I tried calling her as soon as I left the salon but it was just going straight to voicemail. When I got to the pub I couldn't help but smile, I was feeling the happiest I had ever felt. Jack was working that day and he seemed really happy to see me. I was happy to see him too.

"How was your day?" he said, passing me a beer. I sat at the end of the bar, it was pretty empty but I wanted to sit and talk to Jack.

"I had the best day actually, I got a job." I said, struggling to hide my excitement.

"Nice one, where?" Jack seemed genuinely interested in me and it felt nice.

"Hair and Beauty by Vanessa."

"You're kidding? That's like the best salon ever."

"I know."

"So you're a hair stylist then?"

"Not exactly, I'll be working at the reception desk."

"That's amazing, well done you."

"Thanks Jack."

"You know, tell me to get lost if you want but I finish in an hour? If you fancy, maybe go for something to eat?" I was

hesitant but thought what the heck.
"Yes, I would really like that."

At that moment I was so happy, so content. I had my little bedsit, I had Sandra, a new job and I felt like Jack was something special too. I had nothing to lose. I sat at the bar and waited for Jack to finish his shift. I couldn't help but smile at him whilst he was working, he smiled back, shaking his head, laughing to himself. We were like school children, both a little giddy. I tried phoning Sandra whilst I waited but she just wasn't picking up. I knew she hadn't been feeling well so I assumed that she would be resting or in bed. So I decided to send her another message and leave her alone.

ZOE:
Tried calling you again, have some news I want to tell you! Ring me soon as you can, I hope you're feeling better. X

Jack took me to a pizza place in the centre of Manchester, it was busy inside but we managed to get a table. I wasn't used to being taken out, I wasn't even used to eating out. I was entering this world that I had no idea actually could exist with me in it. It was such a nice feeling to feel like I was part of society, after my entire life feeling like a complete waste of space. It wasn't awkward with Jack, it felt natural and real. He was easy to talk to, he was nice to be around.

"Are you sure this place is alright?" Jack said, looking around at all the people, while fiddling with the menu.

"Yes of course it is. I love pizza."

"That's good, because I think that's all this place does." We both laughed and looked over the menu. Whilst we were ordering our drinks and food, my phone started going off. It was a message from Sandra.

SANDRA:
Hey love, sorry been in and out of sleep most of the day. Can't wait to hear your news, can we speak tomorrow morning? I'll ring you.

ZOE:
Yes!! I am out with Jack from the pub, we are having dinner;) x

SANDRA:
Go get him girl! He's fit x

ZOE:
Behave. Speak tomorrow x

SANDRA:
Enjoy your night love, you deserve this x

"Sorry, that was Sandra." I said, putting my phone out of sight.

"The woman you sometimes come into the pub with?"

"Yeah, she's not been feeling well, but I'm speaking with her tomorrow."

"How do you two know each other?" Jack asked, completely genuine, I didn't know what to say.

I was hesitant when I said yes to going for dinner with Jack. I didn't for one second think about all the questions he would be asking me though. I didn't want to lie to him but I felt like that time wasn't the right time to tell him the truth either.

"She was one of my old managers."
"Oh right, nice, you two seem close."
"Yeah, yeah we are."
"I thought she was your mum." he said, not really giving what he said a second thought. I didn't know how to respond, so I just laughed it off.
"How old are you?" I asked him.
"25, you?"
"18."
"You cool with the age gap?"
"Sandra's in her 50's. It's kind of normal for me to have older friends."
"Friends hey? That's what we are?" he smirked.
"Of course."
"Friends are good... for now," he joked. I knew what he was getting at, but he was just a friend. My life was already complicated and it was going to get a whole lot worse. I didn't need any distractions but I actually did have a really nice meal with Jack that day. There were

moments when he asked about my home and family life, I just said that everything was normal and fine, that there was nothing much to say. I did feel like I wanted to tell Jack more but I just didn't know how. He was so kind and caring, he was like no one I had ever met before. He even walked me home and gave me a hug. I could tell that he liked me, I mean I had no experience at all with guys, but he was so warm towards me, he wanted to be around me. I had never had anything like that before, it was really special.

I was excited to speak to Sandra, she was calling me that morning at 9am. I was pacing my bedsit, waiting for the phone to ring. When it did, I rushed over to it on my bed and couldn't wait to tell her everything.

ZOE:
"Hello." I yelled with excitement.
SANDRA:
"Hi love, right go on then."
ZOE:
"I got the job, I start today!"
SANDRA:
Sandra screamed down the phone.
"I am so proud of you Zoe. I knew you could do it."
ZOE:
"She's scary, Vanessa. But I was like a different person."
SANDRA:

"You're getting your confidence girl, I knew you could do it."

ZOE:
"How are you? Are you feeling better?"

SANDRA:
"I'll be fine."

ZOE:
"When can I see you?"

SANDRA:
"Message me later after your shift and we can arrange something. What time do you start?"

ZOE:
"I'm not sure, someone's going to ring me today."

SANDRA:
"Well good luck, speak soon."

ZOE:
"Thank you, have a good day." I threw my phone on my bed and got myself ready. That day was the start of everything, the real beginning of the journey to discover who I was and where I came from, there was no going back.

I got the call to go into the salon at around 11am by one of the stylists, Amy. When I arrived I discovered that Amy was in fact the young girl with the bob, she was ready to meet me and start my induction. Amy took me to a small room at the back of the salon. I couldn't believe I had a job, it was so unreal to me. Amy was really nice, friendly, approachable, she went over all the relevant paperwork and information with me. The job itself was a receptionist role, doing basic admin tasks, helping open up and close down, part time hours over 3 days, Tuesday, Wednesday including a Saturday, 30 minutes for lunch, £10.00ph start. It all sounded fantastic. I was just so grateful for the chance to show what I could do. I just had to remember the real reason why I was there.

I must have only been there for about an hour when I heard Vanessa outside with some clients, she was catching up with them, asking how they were, how their families were, the usual kind of thing. Not long after she stuck her head around the door.

"Why isn't Zoe already on the receptionist desk?"

"I was just..." Amy tried to respond.

"Now please." Vanessa didn't even look at me.

I really enjoyed my first day, although I only saw Vanessa when she stuck her head in. I picked up everything I needed to know quickly and enjoyed the job itself. I loved meeting and greeting everyone. I got a real sense of achievement talking to them, showing an interest in their lives. The people that came into the salon were all on a different level to what I was used to. They were all someone in society, they were important, they had important jobs, important, meaningful lives. I found them interesting, I was fascinated. I wanted to know everything there was about the upper class lifestyle. I wanted to learn and I wanted to fit in. All the staff were so welcoming too, like one big family. They all added me to their social media pages before I left and I remember hoping that we would all become really good friends, that I would finally be able to make good memories, and to have a good life. This was the start of a new chapter, it was going to be one to remember.

I met Sandra that night in our local pub for a catch up. Jack was working and he was all smiles when he saw me walk in.

"Take a seat ladies." he said, whilst pouring us a beer. It was a Tuesday so it wasn't that busy. We got a table in the window and I was just so happy to be with Sandra, I felt good with her, I looked up to her, I really appreciated her in my life.

"Here's to you darling." Sandra said, raising her glass to mine.

"So how was your first day?"

"Yeah it was good, I loved it, I only saw Vanessa once, she didn't even react to me."

"Don't worry, she's noticing you."

"My interview was unreal, I felt like she was testing me."

"She will be, you have just turned up and she's interested in you, this little girl with all this confidence and sassiness."

"I worry sometimes."

"What about?"

"Losing myself in this pretend life, because that's what it is, pretend. I am not the girl I am making out to be."

"You listen to me. You are doing this for the most genuine reason there is, you want/need to know the truth. You are going to do whatever it takes, okay? And don't worry, I won't let you lose yourself."

"Thank you. How are you feeling?"

"Yeah, better. I have a doctor's appointment next week though, my stomach's been hurting, probably an infection or something."

"Can I come with you?"

"Don't be daft, I'm fine. Anyway, what about you two?" Sandra said, with a smirk on her face looking over to Jack behind the bar.

"There is no- us- we went for dinner, it was nice, that's it." Sandra got up from her seat and rushed to the bar, I watched her talk to Jack, he looked over to me and smiled. I was so confused. What was she doing? Sandra came back a few minutes later and dropped a piece of paper in front of me.

"His number, life is short Zoe, you like each other, nothing to lose."

"But."

"No, do as you're told." I took the piece of paper, smiled at Sandra and then looked over to Jack and smirked.

"Don't lose it." Jack shouted over. I spent most of that night with Sandra, when Jack finished his shift he joined us and the three of us did nothing but laugh. I couldn't believe how in such a small space of time, I had a home, a job, friends, Sandra who was like family to me and a special friend in Jack. My life was becoming something I was proud of, trouble is, it wasn't real.

Chapter 7
A Girl Called Megan

Almost a month had passed, time seemed to just fly by, I was busy with work and socialising. My life was getting hectic and I loved it. I had settled well into my job, I knew how to do everything that I needed to and I was well liked by the other staff members and the clients. I was earning good money and started to save a little bit, I had created a whole new life. My bedsit never looked better, I had bought a new wardrobe with all my designer clothes neatly placed on silver coat hangers. I bought new red curtains to match my bedding and a fluffy red rug. I had 2 glass vases in my window with the most beautiful fresh flowers. I got rid of the small table that was in the kitchen and bought a breakfast bar with two stools. Everything in the kitchen matched, I chose a green colour bread bin, kettle, cups, towels. The bathroom was full of pink towels, matching rugs, I had candles everywhere, it was like a show home, everything neat, tidy and had a place. I was so proud of it, I loved being at home. I had never said that in my life, but it felt amazing to have somewhere I felt I belonged.

I saw a lot of Jack because most days I would go into the pub and chat with him whilst having a few beers. We had been out for a few meals together by that point and it was always fun. I hadn't opened up to him much about anything but we enjoyed spending time together, we messaged all the time and it was comforting knowing he was there. I hadn't seen much of Sandra, we messaged all the time but she still wasn't feeling well with her infection she had. I just thought she was taking a bit of time off work to recover. Not much had happened in regards to Vanessa, she had started to acknowledge me at work, she would give me the odd smile but I hadn't had any real or proper conversations with her.

It was a Wednesday morning, the most beautiful sunny day in Manchester. I started work at 9am sharp. I headed to a coffee shop I had started to go to every morning, joining in the hustle and bustle of everyone going about their day. I loved having a routine. When I got to work, Amy had already started opening up the salon. I absolutely loved that job, I felt so important, so relevant, like I actually mattered. I felt proud, like I finally belonged. By that time I was more then able to do the job on my own, stylists would come in and set up ready for the day, Amy would open up, get all her PR work from the reception desk and head over to the back to start her day and I was already to go on the reception. I adored being front of house, speaking to everyone, essentially I was the face of the salon, it felt great.

It was that Wednesday morning when something happened that I wasn't expecting, wasn't expecting it at all. I was behind the reception desk, answering emails about bookings, answering the phone, doing all the admin tasks. The salon was busy with clients and stylists getting on with their work, coffee was flowing and for those clients who wanted it, a glass of champagne or two. I was always told that every time the salon door opened, you needed to stand up and be ready to give the biggest welcome possible. I heard the door go and a woman walked in, she looked at me and smiled before walking into the salon. I was taken back, she seemed to know where she was going. Do I stop her? I wasn't sure. This woman was beautiful, mid thirties, brown curly hair, shoulder length, tied back with a green bobble. I noticed her long grey coat almost touching the floor, tied in the middle wearing the most petite small heel grey boots. Before I had a chance to follow her, one of the stylists saw me looking and came over.

"Don't worry, that's Vanessa's daughter," he said.

"What?"

"Well daughter in law, but they are so close, she comes and goes as she pleases, she gets free everything, just so you know. Don't look so worried, you did fine." he walked back over to his client. I was still, standing frozen, thinking about what he had just said to me. So Vanessa didn't have a daughter? She had a daughter in law? What the hell was going on? I watched as this woman made her way round to the back of the salon,

"Vanessa isn't in at the moment." Amy said, offering the woman a coffee.

"Thanks Hun, I'll just wait for her in her office."

"Excuse me, Excuse me." A client was trying to get my attention.

"Sorry, how can I help?" I said, my mind wondering.

"Can I pay please." I dealt with the client and sat back down in the chair. I couldn't focus, I couldn't concentrate. I wanted to go and talk to this woman but I knew I couldn't, so I just sat with anticipation. About twenty minutes passed and in walked Vanessa, all done up, fresh curly hair, red dress, black coat and boots, her entrance as bold as her outfit, she had an awe about her, controlling the entire room with her no nonsense approach to anything.

"Morning babe." she said to me rushing past the desk.

"Megan's waiting for you." Amy said to her.

So I found out this woman was called Megan, and she was in fact Vanessa's daughter in law. Right, okay.

"Hello my sweetheart." I heard Vanessa say.

"Mum, so good to see you, you look amazing." I heard them laughing and joking, they were clearly very close. I felt sick to the stomach, my entire body had pins and needles, my hands were sweaty, I felt like I couldn't breathe. I ran to the bathroom, everyone saw and everyone was worried. Amy followed me offering support.

"Are you alright?" I couldn't answer, I was trying so hard to control my breathing. I couldn't let Vanessa see me like that, she might have remembered the panic attack I had in The Latte House. I had to be so careful.

"Zoe." Amy said, with concern.

"I'm alright, honest, please just give me five minutes."

"Of course, I'll cover reception."

When I heard Amy leave, I opened the cubicle door and stood over the sink. I slowly looked up to the mirror, this blonde straight haired, smokey eyed girl with the most beautiful silk, black dress with red stripes was staring back. Tears filled my eyes so much that my reflection started to look distorted. I might have looked confident, sassy, stylish, but inside I was still that eighteen year old girl in the worn out green hoodie stood in my bedsit, wanting to belong, to fit in, to be loved. How could I ever compete with what Vanessa and Megan had? Megan was clearly the daughter Vanessa always wanted. How did she know that I wouldn't have been what she wanted though? I was just a baby, a newborn baby. I wiped my tears with some paper towels and headed for the door.

"Oh sorry." I said, I wasn't looking where I was going and had bumped into someone. When I looked up from wiping my eyes it was Megan.

"It's fine, you alright Hun?" Megan said. I nodded and quickly went over to Amy to take over reception. Not long after Vanessa and Megan were leaving the salon together.

"I probably won't be back today." Vanessa said to me as she left.

74

"Nice to meet you." Megan made a point of saying to me as she held the salon door open for them. I smiled at her and watched them both leave until they were out of sight. There was only one person I wanted right then...Sandra.

On my break I messaged Sandra asking if we could meet. It didn't take her long to respond, she said it would be really nice to see me but she didn't want to go out, so she invited me round to her house in Salford. I couldn't wait to see her, she messaged me the address and as soon as it got to 4pm, I got a taxi to her house. I was in the taxi for about half an hour when it pulled up in a cul-de-sac. The street was really nice, the houses only looked small but they were all well looked after. All the same colour brick work with small front gardens, most covered with flowers. I walked round the small street until I got to number 8. I walked up the small patio path and knocked on the door.

"It's open!" I could hear Sandra shouting. I let myself in and Sandra came rushing from the kitchen to greet me, she gave me the biggest hug and I just broke down.

"Darling, what's happened?" She took me in her arms into the front room and sat me on the sofa, she sat next to me, her arms still wrapped around me.

"I've got you, let it out." I pulled away, my hair a mess, eyes soaked with tears.

"I met this woman today called Megan. Apparently she's Vanessa's daughter in law."

"Daughter in law?"

"Yes, one of the stylists said that Vanessa sees her as a daughter. I mean you could see how close they are, but anyway Vanessa doesn't actually have a daughter!"

"None of this makes any sense!"

"I spoke to her, she seemed nice, she's so beautiful."

"Of course she is, who isn't there."

"What am I meant to do now?"

"Honestly love, I really don't know." Sandra sighed heavily, kissed my cheek and left to the kitchen, wiping my eyes yet again I looked around her home. It was everything I expected it to be, the walls were all painted white and covered in pictures of what I assume was her family, some pictures were on canvases, others in frames, all scattered around the walls, some big, some small. Green drape curtains hung from the front window looking out onto the front garden. A 2 seater, black, leather sofa sat underneath the window, I sat on a 3 seater sofa to match to the left, they were covered in green cushions and throws. It was all open planned, the TV was in front of me on a glass cabinet and further on down the room was a small 4 person table and chairs, there were double doors at the back leading out onto some lawn. It was cosy and it was a home, something I always dreamed of having.

All of a sudden I heard coughing in the back, an intense coughing.

"Sandra. You alright?" There was no response. I went to look for her, I walked back out the living room door, to the right of me was the front door, to the left were stairs leading upstairs then next to me was a small corridor to the kitchen. I headed for the kitchen, when I got to the doorway Sandra was standing over the sink, as if she was about to throw up.

"Oh my god, are you alright?" I rushed over to her, taking a glass from the side and filling it with water. I helped her drink it.

"Stop fussing, I'm fine. Go and wait in the front room."

"But."

"Now!!" she shouted. I did what she said and waited. I know the feeling of wanting to be left alone when you're throwing up so I didn't think too much into it. Not long after Sandra came back to me.

"Sorry about that love." she said, sitting next to me with some tea and biscuits she had made for us.

"Are you alright?" I was worried about her. Sandra kissed my forehead, took my hand and got comfy in her seat.

"I am going to be strict with you now Zoe." I was worried when she said that, but I kept quiet and I listened.

"You need to do more love, you have been working there for about a month now, you need to be getting closer to Vanessa."

"It's hard, she's hard to get close to."

"You can't get too settled, remember we are doing this to find out what happened to you, not for you to be the next best hair stylist, that dream is never going to happen."

"I know it's not real, but it's nice, for the first time I belong."

"Awe Zoe, you'll always belong my love, you'll always belong with me. But we don't have time to waste. We need to move with this now. When are you next at work?"

"Saturday."

"Right, Saturday. Leave it with me."

"What does that mean?"

"Trust me, okay? Now have some tea."

"Sandra?"

"Yes."

"Can I stay with you tonight?"

"You don't even need to ask."

I took off my shoes and curled into a ball resting my head on Sandra's lap, she put her hand on my head and started playing with my hair. I felt myself drift off and suddenly it was black.

Chapter 8
Baby Drama

The chat with Sandra really stuck in my head, she was so adamant with what I needed to do, I often thought about what I would have done without her. I trusted Sandra, I knew she was genuine. I could tell just how much she cared about me, I think we were always meant to meet each other, our paths were always going to cross. I remembered what Sandra had said about needing to move forward with Vanessa, get her to notice me more. But I was nervous, Vanessa was scary, intimidating, a strong, confident, successful business woman, the opposite to me. I didn't know what to do, what to say. I paced the salon, trying to look for answers. I just didn't want to sabotage my job before it had really begun, I still hadn't been there that long. I thought keeping my head down for a good few months would be the right way forward, but Sandra assured me that this was something that needed to happen now. I heard the door open behind me, the sound of the bell ringing through the salon.

"Morning." it was Amy, she was on an early shift too.

"Oh morning." I said, surprised to see her. I decided to use the opportunity to try and get some information.

"It was nice the other day, seeing Vanessa with Megan." I said, switching on some lights behind one of the display units. Amy was fiddling with the computer behind the reception desk.

"Yeah, Megan is lovely."

"Does Megan often come to the salon?"

"She used to come all the time but not as much any more."

"Oh right."

"Chloe keeps her occupied."

"Chloe?"

"Megan's daughter." Amy said, taking off her coat to hang up. I couldn't believe it, I almost knocked some products off the unit, as I leant on it thinking about what Amy had just said. Vanessa really did have the perfect little family didn't she? Every time I found out something, it made me feel worse, not better. Maybe this was a mistake? What on earth was I doing?

I was so angry. It really started to affect me, how could it not? I was slowly starting to discover who I was, where I came from and it was looking like I literally was just tossed to the side and forgot about. I must have been a really bad, ugly, disgusting baby. What did I do so wrong? I couldn't get my head around it. The other stylists arrived, setting up their work stations, clients all wanting warm welcomes, but I was so angry at the point I couldn't even pretend. I could tell that people were noticing but do you know what, I didn't care. I was so blaise that I hadn't even noticed Vanessa had just walked in.

"Zoe! Zoe! Zoe!" The shouting got louder, it caught my attention. I snapped out of my commoditised state to Vanessa stood in front of me, looking very tense. She was leaning on the reception desk with authority.

"Come with me, now! Amy take over." Vanessa led the way to her office, her heels making the loudest sound, her heels were all you could ever hear in the salon. I followed her with anticipation.

"Sit down." she sternly said, taking off her black fur coat and draping it over one of the chairs. I did what she asked and clutched my hands, they were clammy and I could feel myself going red. I heard Vanessa shut the door behind me, that loud, harsh sound it made was chilling. She slowly walked around me and sat down on the chair in front of me.

"What the hell are you playing at?" she said, sitting back in her chair, folding her arms. I went numb. I didn't know what to say.

"You do know you're still on probation? I don't expect clients to come to my salon and get a half-arsed welcome." I still said nothing.

"Zoe, are you even listening to me? You know what I think we are done here." I could feel Vanessa losing patience with me. I couldn't lose that job, lose that connection with her, I needed it so bad, I didn't mean to say it but I panicked.

"I'm pregnant." I blurted out.

Silence. Vanessa stared at me, my face was hot with anxiety, tears started to fill my eyes, more so because I was thinking... Why the hell did I just say that?

"Don't worry, it's not your problem."I rushed to get up.
"Don't move. You're not going anywhere." Vanessa said.
"When did you find out?" I knew what I had to do now, I had no choice. If I ever was going to find out my truth, I needed to lie.
"Last night, I was late for my period."
"Does the dad know?"
"No. I'm not with anyone, it just happened."
"Silly girl. Well that explains your recent behaviour, I'm willing to overlook it this once." I felt like Vanessa was almost done with me and was just going to send me straight back to work with not a care in the world. So I just kept digging that hole.

"I don't want it." I said, looking away to the floor.
"I beg your pardon?" My words had clearly got to her.
"I don't want it." I repeated.
"I think you need to talk to your mum."
"I don't have a mum."
"What?"
"I don't have a mum, I don't have anyone?"
"Don't be ridiculous, you must have someone you can talk to?" I shook my head feeling sorry for myself.

"I was brought up in care, I'm alone." Vanessa's body language changed, she seemed more open to me, she uncrossed her arms and leant forward in her chair, she studied me for a while.

"I'm sorry I had no idea." she said, almost looking guilty for how she had spoken to me in the past. I nodded.

"Will you help me?" I said, a little desperate.

"Help you?" Vanessa looked puzzled.

"I want to get rid of it." I clutched my hands with the guilt of all the lies I was telling.

"Zoe, you cannot ask me that. I can't. I won't."

"Okay. Can I go back to work please." I said, avoiding eye contact- almost monotone. My cheeks were wet with tears. Vanessa didn't respond but I felt at that time that I could leave. When the door closed behind me I felt sick to the stomach. What was I doing?

I went over to Amy, who could tell I had been crying, she didn't say anything but she put her arm around me as she got up to leave me at the reception area. I collapsed in my chair and got on with my job. I kept thinking at least I still had the job, and I did speak to Vanessa on a more personal level too, so I was hoping that was a positive step forward, even if I did have to tell the most horrible lie to get there.

About half an hour later I saw Vanessa go and talk to Amy. Amy kept looking over in my direction which made me extremely paranoid. Vanessa had her big, black, fur coat on, she was clearly leaving. Oh well at least I tried.

Vanessa walked over to me.

"Amy is working the rest of your shift, come with me."

"What? Where?" I asked, in a bit of a panic.

"Now Zoe." Vanessa held open the salon door for me to walk out first, everyone looked on with curiosity wondering what was going on. I grabbed my coat and bag and headed for the door. I was terrified. Where were we going? What was she going to do? I followed her, unsure of everything.

Chapter 9
It's All About The Lies

It was warm, really warm. I don't think it was the place we were in, or because of the weather. I think I was so warm, so hot, so flustered because of the stress, tension and panic I felt with the situation I had found myself in. We were back in The Latte House. I was so worried that she would recognise me from when I had the panic attack there. I knew I looked really different by that point, but I was still the same girl inside. I was terrified. Vanessa was in the bathroom, probably powdering her nose. I sat on the edge of my chair, patiently waiting. "Latte and a bottle of water." Vanessa came out of the bathroom and shouted over to the staff, who were only too happy to help. It wasn't very busy, and even if it was, I still think the staff would have dropped anything that they were doing to accommodate Vanessa, people were in awe of her. They wanted her to talk to them, they wanted to be around her and they wanted her approval. She took off her coat, fiddled with her phone for a bit before placing it down on the table. I didn't look at her, I almost started believing my own lie, feeling really shit about the pretend abortion that I wanted.
"Yes. I will help you." Vanessa suddenly said. Before I could react the waiter was bringing over our drinks she

had ordered for us. Vanessa took the bottle of water, unscrewed the lid and gave it to me.

"Drink it all. You look terrible." she said, whilst opening a sweetener to put into her latte. I took a massive gulp, I was beyond thirsty.

"I will book you the appointment you need at my doctors. They are the best out there. I will take you and stay with you. We will do it as soon as we can. It's best not to think about it too much. It will be all over by next week." She took a sip of her latte.

"I need to…" I got up and ran to the bathroom. I collapsed in the same cubicle as before and constantly started to throw up. I had just lied about being pregnant, I had just lied about needing an abortion, and I didn't know what to do next. I felt trapped. I got myself together and left the cubicle, I stood by the sink in front of the mirror, looking at my reflection, I did not recognise myself. I took some paper towels from the rack at the side and I wiped under my eyes. What kind of person was I becoming? I felt like I literally was creating a monster.

When I went back out to Vanessa, she was sitting staring ahead, with her drink in her hands. I sat down and shuffled my chair close to the table.

"Thank you." I just about managed to say.

"Finish your water." Vanessa finished her drink, she then went into her handbag and took a small, white card out, she handed it to me.

"The number at the bottom is my personal number, save it and I will message you the appointment details." I took it and held it in front of me, tears falling down my cheeks, I nodded. Vanessa put on her coat before dropping some money with the waiter for our drinks and then she just left. I hung my head in my hands. The only person I wanted with me was Sandra.

"Thank you." I said to the waiter, whilst rushing past him to leave. I needed some air, when I got outside I looked up at the sky and took the deepest breath possible. It felt so good to feel the wind on my skin, I stayed there for a good few seconds before taking my phone out of my pocket to ring Sandra. I really needed to talk to her.

ZOE:
"It's me."
SANDRA:
"How did it go?" I couldn't answer her, I just burst into tears.
"Come stay with me again love." Sandra said, concerned about me and wanting to help. I put down the phone and flagged a passing taxi to take me to Sandra's house.

We sat in silence on the sofa, the ticking of the clock is the only sound that could be heard.
"Right, spit it out." Sandra said, agitated at the awkward silences. I looked at her, disappointed in myself.
"I had to say it, I was going to lose my job."

"Had to say what?"

"I told her I was pregnant."

"WHAT!"

"I wanted her to feel sorry for me, so she would let me in a bit, you know talk to me on a personal level like you said."

"But pregnant? What are you going to do when there's no bump and no baby?" I went quiet not wanting to tell Sandra anymore.

"Zoe there's more isn't there?"

"I told her... I wanted an abortion."

"Oh this just gets better."

"I panicked."

"You think."

"Look I'm sorry, I messed up but I found out that Megan..."

"Megan?"

"Vanessa's daughter in law, well she has a daughter-Chloe. Vanessa literally has this perfect little family."

"Awe Zoe."

"I couldn't focus! People at work noticed and Vanessa took me to her office, she would have fired me Sandra. I didn't know what to do, I didn't know what to say, I..."

"Calm down!" Sandra yelled.

I remember how useless I felt, there was no way I could keep it up, it was all getting too messy. Things were getting serious, really serious.

"What happened after you told her that?"

"Nothing at first, I asked her to help me but she just sent me back to work. Then a bit later on she got Amy to cover my shift and she took me to a coffee shop."

"Bloody hell."

"She said she's going to make an appointment, you know, to get rid of the baby."

"Zoe! There is no bloody baby!"

"Yes I know. I'm just telling you what she said."

"Well you are just going to have to go through with it until the appointment and then… I don't know, say you made a mistake, you come on your period or something."

"But I can't…"

"Can't what? Lie? Yes, you can. And you will."

"I'm sorry, I know I've messed up."

"Come here." Sandra wrapped her arms around me.

"This is serious stuff what you're saying Zoe, you need to be careful." I squeezed Sandra tight, just as I did, my phone went off. I pulled away from her slowly, looking at her as I took my phone from my pocket. It was a message from Vanessa.

VANESSA:
Appointment is at 2.45pm next Tuesday. Meet me at The Latte House, a driver will take us there and drop us back. Vanessa.

"Not one for words, Vanessa is she?" Sandra said, whilst holding my phone, reading the message.

"Well at least you don't have to keep this up long." she continued.

"What shall I do?"

"You do nothing tonight. Tomorrow send her a message back, asking if you can see her, you are worried, you want to talk. Get over it now Zoe, it's done. Next week this lie will be put to bed... in a fashion, we need to focus on the task in hand, okay?"

"Yes okay." Sandra sat back on the sofa and held her arms open for me to lay on her, I did just that, she was like the mother I always wanted.

"I don't know what I would do without you." I said, holding on to her with all I had.

"Enough of that silly girl." she said, softly, her arms holding me that little bit tighter.

The next morning I woke at 3am to Sandra, she was violently coughing and throwing up. I rushed to the bathroom to see if she was alright, but the door was locked. I banged on it a few times.

"Sandra, you alright?"

"Yes, go back to bed." I was starting to worry about her, she had been back and forth to the doctors and they had said it was just a cold but if you heard her coughing! It was painful to listen to. I got back into my bed and stared at the ceiling, my mind thinking about Vanessa, wondering how I was going to tell her the truth. The truth that I wasn't pregnant, that there was no baby without coming across like a horrible, little liar. I took my phone from the bedside table and spontaneously sent her a message.

ZOE:
I really need to talk to you. Can we meet ASAP?

I quickly put my phone back down on the table and turned away from it, pulling the covers over my head. I just wanted to get that part of my life over with. I was creating more and more drama but I didn't know how else to play it. At that moment when I thought Vanessa was going to fire me and all of my hard work would have been for nothing, I thought the shock factor would be the best thing to do. I needed her to listen to me and to feel sorry for me, but I never for one second thought about the seriousness of the lie itself. I guess there are some things you should never lie about? But I mean, I was desperate.

I went downstairs a few hours later and Sandra was sitting in the kitchen, in her pink, fluffy dressing gown looking through some photos. There was a large green cup in front of her of fresh tea that she had just poured herself, from her funky looking whale shaped teapot. There was steam coming from the top of her mug.
"I couldn't sleep." I said, taking a seat next to her.
"Me neither." Sandra got up and took another cup from the side, she passed it to me and I poured myself some tea.
"Are you sure you're alright?" I said, genuinely concerned.
"Yes, now stop asking."

91

"What's all this?"

"This, this is my life." Sandra said, moving her hand over all the photos.

"Can I see?"

"Of course." Sandra held up a photo so I could see it more clearly.

"This is my husband and my son." The picture was of the three of them outside a caravan, they were all laughing. Her son only looked little.

"This was taken on one of our little weekend breaks to Yorkshire, we saved up for years to be able to rent that caravan. We loved it, by the sea.

"You look so happy."

"I was, we were"

"What happened?"

"Life."

"What do you mean?"

"I got old." Sandra didn't need to say anymore, I got what she meant from the tone of her voice and the way she rushed to put the picture out of sight.

"Maybe you should reach out to your son, go see him."

"He knows where I am, he's too busy for his old mum now. Anyway I've got you, you keep me busy." she said, whilst holding onto my cheek. I smiled, nodding.

"I sent Vanessa a message early this morning, telling her I needed to see her."

"Good, that's good."

"She hasn't replied yet."

"It's not even 7am Zoe, she will, don't worry."
"Right more tea?"
I watched Sandra struggle to pour herself some more tea, something wasn't right.

Vanessa did eventually reply to my message. I made my way over to The Latte House which is where Vanessa told me to meet her. I was very apprehensive because I had no idea what I was actually going to say. I felt nervous the closer the taxi got to dropping me off.
"Thank you." I said, to the taxi driver as I struggled to undo the seat-belt that was tight around me.
When I arrived she was already sitting down waiting for me in her usual seat, that domineering look she would always give me was stronger than ever. I took a deep breath and walked over to her. I could feel my hands sweating as I moved the chair to sit down. I could barely look at her. I could feel her staring intensely at me.
"I'm sorry." I was barely able to articulate my words. Vanessa leant forward.
"Sorry about what? Zoe, look at me?" she said, cold and distant.
"There is no baby." I quickly said, hoping the floor would swallow me whole. Vanessa sat back with a look of confusion.
"I don't understand. You've already had the abortion?" Vanessa was trying to figure out what the hell I was talking about.

"I was never pregnant. I've had a period, I just panicked, sorry." I said, my face wet with tears. Vanessa reached for her handbag and placed it on her lap, she stared at me for a few moments before standing up, she placed her hand on my shoulder.

"You'll be alright darling, I will cancel your appointment." she almost looked relieved that she didn't have to help me anymore. I was glad when she left to be honest, she was like added pressure on top of everything else. I didn't find it any easier to talk to her or to be around her, and she still didn't seem to want to get to know me in the way that I had hoped. Vanessa was completely different with Megan, she was maternal, so I knew she had it in her. Maybe she just didn't like me?

I gathered myself together and headed to The Plant Pot. When I walked in Jack was standing at the bar, he had just finished his shift, his eyes lit up when he saw me.

"Hello stranger." he said, rushing up to give me a hug.

"Hey." I was a little tense, I couldn't help it, I couldn't hold back any longer, I just sobbed.

"Hey babe, it's alright, I've got you." Jack held me and took me over to a table hidden behind some new notice boards that the pub just had delivered. The other barman who was talking to Jack when I arrived (I didn't catch his name) just left us to it.

"This is embarrassing." I said, trying to stop myself from crying and my makeup going everywhere. Jack just looked at me with a concerned expression.

"Why do you like me?" I asked him, I could sense that he would do anything for me and I didn't know why. I wasn't anything special. He didn't even know who I really was. Everything was just one big lie.

"You light up the room when you smile, you're beautiful Zoe." When he said those things to me, I couldn't help but smile. I knew Jack was 'the one'. I just couldn't tell him, not then. It wasn't the right time. I thought I had all the time in the world, I didn't know it then but my time was the one thing I was running out of. And I was running out of it fast.

Chapter 10
Keeping Up Appearances

It was like nothing had ever happened at work, in fact it seemed like Vanessa had completely erased it all from her memory. I know none of it was true but I still felt like I had to keep up the pretence. I just needed Vanessa to reach out to me, to want to be there for me, I needed her to like me, to like me so much that she would want to go out of her way to make sure I was alright. I just had no idea of how to do it.

I was quiet at work, I kept myself to myself my first few shifts back after talking to Vanessa at The Latte House. I still did my job well, but there was no spark there, my mind was always preoccupied on other things, people could definitely tell there was something wrong, staff and clients, I couldn't help it. I tried my best to just 'get on with it' but it was easier said than done.

One morning whilst I was opening up, I was surprised to see Megan walk through the salon door, she was clearly upset, she had been crying, her cheeks were wet and her eyes were watery. I stopped what I was doing and turned around to her.
"Megan what is it?" I said, feeling a little out of place with her, but there was no one else there and she was upset so I tried to help. Megan just looked at me and shook her

head, holding her hands to her face and taking the deepest breath.

"Can I get you some water?" Megan nodded whilst she took a seat in the waiting area. I went to the water dispenser and filled a small plastic cup of ice cold water. I caught Megan's reflection in one of the mirrors, she just kept crying and crying.

"There you go." I said, passing her the water.

"Thanks." she took a sip whilst I stood awkwardly not knowing what to do.

"Sit down." Megan said, suggesting I sit next to her.

"You haven't been here long, have you?" I shook my head.

"I'm sorry for being such a mess."

"What's happened?" I was intrigued and wanted to know why Vanessa's daughter in law was in such a state, and Vanessa was nowhere to be seen.

"Shall I call Vanessa for you."

"NO!" Megan grabbed hold of my arm with force.

"I don't want Vanessa, okay?"

"Yes okay." I said, pulling my arm away.

"I thought you two were close." Megan looked at me and laughed sarcastically before finishing her water.

"We are sometimes too close."

"Maybe you could talk to your mum about it?" I asked.

"I don't have a mum, well not anymore."

"I'm so sorry, I shouldn't have..."

"No it's alright, my parents spent more time in prison than at home with me, I haven't a clue where they are now."

"Oh I'm sorry."

"Zoe stop apologising. I don't mind talking about it."

"I don't have anyone either." I said, without realising what I was actually saying. I had to be so careful with what I told people but for the first time since working for Vanessa, that felt the most real and genuine chat I could have hoped for.

"What do you mean?" Megan said, her eyes had started to stop crying, she turned to me on the sofa we were sitting on.

"I was abandoned as a baby, brought up in care, I don't have any family." I said, reflecting on my words. It did still hurt me, but I became numb to it the older I got. Now all I wanted and needed were answers. Megan looked at me in disbelief, she looked genuinely sorry for me, for what I had been through. All of a sudden Megan wrapped her arms around me. I can't describe the warm feeling I got when she held me, it was like everything just stopped, everything paused in that one moment. I closed my eyes and let her hold me tighter and tighter, lost in her brown fluffy coat, I could smell her perfume. The fresh and captivating scent of rose and jasmine. It was one of those moments that I knew I would never forget. All of a sudden there was the sound of the door swinging open and the bell ringing which made us both jump.

"What's going on?" It was Vanessa. Megan pulled away from me and I quickly stood up. None of us spoke. Vanessa slowly walked closer to us, her heels were all we could hear, her long mustard coat was almost touching the floor, her eyes covered with black designer glasses and the biggest blow-dry possible, she stopped directly at the side of the sofa, towering over Megan.

"Well?" she repeated. I looked at Megan, who looked at me and winked before brushing herself off and standing up.

"I was just inviting Zoe to my 33rd birthday party on Saturday." I was gobsmacked. Was this for real? Me? Invited to Megan's birthday? Vanessa looked confused too.

"Oh and for the 100th time, I want MY birthday party at MY house, not YOURS! Everyone knows you have a swimming pool Vanessa." Megan said, whilst walking out the salon. I couldn't believe that Megan had just spoken to Vanessa like that, she was clearly embarrassed that I had witnessed it but in true Vanessa fashion she just looked at me and said.

"Haven't you got work to do?" before walking away from me to go and hide in her office.

What a morning, it wasn't even 9am yet and I had made more progress in the space of half an hour then I had done in two months. I just wished that Vanessa wasn't as cold with me all the time. I started to wonder if maybe she did me a favour after all giving me up? She clearly wasn't maternal, I thought her and Megan had a good, solid relationship but maybe that was all a front, because Megan was really upset with her. If Vanessa was who I thought she was, then she was giving me no signs that she ever wanted to be a mum, none at all. I honestly had never met anyone who was so full of life, lived life to the full but then on an intimate level was so cold and distant, even when she was attempting to help.

The chat with Megan did lift my spirits and I was in a much better mood all day. It just gave me confidence in myself that I was a good person. I was only lying because I was desperate to find out the truth, but that moment with Megan seemed real and it was so sad to see her so upset. I couldn't believe she had invited me to her birthday party either. I was nervous of course I was, going somewhere on my own, where I didn't really know anyone but I wasn't going to back down.

Before the end of my shift I realised that I didn't have a clue where Megan actually lived so I apprehensively went to Vanessa's office. I knocked on her door until I heard her tell me to go in.

"Hi Vanessa." I walked through the door to find Vanessa sitting, surrounded by piles of hair style magazines, she was writing things down on colour post- it notes and attaching them to certain pages of the magazines.

"What is it?" she said, not looking at me.

"Please could I have Megan's address, I'm not sure where to go on Saturday."

"Oh so you're going then?" she said, still fiddling with the post- it notes. I didn't know what she wanted me to say.

"You know Zoe, I must say you do fascinate me?"

Vanessa was still giving me no eye contact. I didn't really understand what she was talking about.

"I'm sorry I don't understand." I said, stood on the spot, not daring to move, already feeling on edge. Vanessa leaned back in her chair and for the first time looked up at me.

"What are you up to?" she asked, folding her arms.

Shit! I said to myself. I didn't say anything to Vanessa, I just stared at her whilst going red in the face.

"Two months ago I had absolutely no idea who you were. You came here with an adequate CV, made quite an impression, thought you were having a baby, been up and down like a yo-yo at reception and now you are coming to my daughter in law's birthday party."

Once she had finished ranting at me. I did think to myself that she was right, so much had happened. I felt at times that I wasn't getting anywhere, Sandra kept telling me that I needed to keep pushing things to find out the truth but actually, I did do a fair bit since moving into my bedsit on that very first day. But right then in that moment I didn't know how to justify what Vanessa was saying to me. Vanessa was so forward, so direct and to the point. I decided that if she was going to fire me, she would do it regardless of my approach so I decided to play her at her own game.

"Why don't you like me?"

"I beg your pardon?"

"What did I ever do wrong for you to hate me?" Vanessa was taken back by my sudden questions that she clearly didn't have answers for.

"I love this job. I'm proud to have this job. Yes you're right, my CV wasn't worthy of working for you, but all I wanted was a chance to try and make something of myself, to be proud of my life. I'm sorry I came to you for help when I thought I was pregnant, I thought you would be?"

"What?" Vanessa interrupted me. "Thought I would be what?"

"I thought you would be kind." I said, looking away from her down to the floor. Vanessa paused for a moment. "Look Zoe, I am sorry for what you have gone through in the past, but I'm not... I'm not your mum."

Yes. I know what you're thinking. Vanessa actually said that. And it did hurt. Those words hurt me so much, I cannot even begin to describe the pain that went through my entire body at that time. I took a deep breath, trying not to break down. After she had said that I didn't want her to see me broken. Vanessa took a post-it note and scribbled something on it, before holding it up to me. I clutched my hands tight beside me before reaching out to take the note. It was Megan's address. I held it in front of me with both hands and nodded, a single tear fell from my eye. "You know Vanessa, I looked up to you, like so many do. You are beautiful and stylish, successful and rich. You're a strong woman. You're also very cold and cruel and for someone with the life you have, I really don't understand why you have so much hate towards me."

I turned my back on her and walked out the room. Vanessa didn't even bother saying anything else to me. I do think she knew that she went too far, saying that she wasn't my mum. If only she knew? The one thing I was certain of when I left that shift was that I was bloody going to Megan's birthday party and I was going in style!

Chapter 11
Megan's Birthday

I met Sandra and Jack in The Plant Pot for a few drinks. Jack was working until 8ish then he was going to take me to a new Italian, that had just opened in town. He loved pizza, he was actually really funny with me, he always made sure that wherever he took me they did pizza. I didn't mind but he didn't think I knew what he was doing, coming up with all these restaurant suggestions spontaneously to me, that he had secretly studied the menu for. Jack was so refreshing, I started to feel excited every time I would be with him. He made me feel like I was the only girl in the world, and with everything going on, I needed that feeling.

Sandra and I sat in our usual spot in the window, watching the world go by. We caught up on the week before and I told her about the moment I had with Megan. Sandra couldn't believe the intense moment I had with Vanessa, let alone that I had been invited to Megan's party. Sandra always supported me, she always had my back, she would tell me if she thought I was doing something wrong and she would praise me if I was doing anything right. It was ironic really, there I was trying to find my real mother, yet for the first time, I felt like I already had one. Sandra had slowly started to fill the piece of my heart that had always been missing. I couldn't thank her enough.

"You still have that cough." I said to Sandra, as she came back from the bar with another round of beers.
"It won't shift. I do feel better though. So what are you going to wear tomorrow?"
"I have no idea." Sandra sat back in her chair like someone had punched her in the back.
"Zoe!" she said, with a rush of adrenaline.
"Yes?"
"The red dress?" Sandra started clapping her hands, looking more than pleased with her suggestion.
"Sandra, it's like a ball gown, I can't wear that."
"Yes you can! You want to make a statement don't you? Well if you wear that, Vanessa won't be able to take her eyes off you."
I wasn't sure but I entertained the idea for a while. I wasn't even sure at that time if I wanted to get closer to Vanessa. I wasn't liking what I was seeing and I wondered if it was even worth my time. Would she even care if she knew who I actually was? I didn't think I was ever that important to her. The reason why she left me as a baby started to become clearer, she didn't want to be MY mother.
"I wonder what type of a mother Vanessa was to her son?" I said to Sandra.
"Honestly, I have no idea."

"She left me as a baby, you know I've never been able to get that out of my head. Vanessa shows no emotional connection to anyone, well not really and yet she has had a baby and brought him up."

"Yes or her servants did." Sandra laughed.

Sandra was right, just because she had a son it didn't mean that she brought him up herself. Maybe she did have help? Maybe she didn't see anything of him? But I still had that question. Even if she was the worst Mum ever, how come she gave him a chance and not me?

"Zoe I have always said that the truth might not be what you want to hear, it might not be the perfect answer you're searching for."

"I know." I sighed. Sandra took hold of my hand that was tightly holding my beer glass.

"I'm here love and so is Jack." I looked over at Jack who was busy taking people's orders. I looked back over to Sandra and smiled.

"Now you're staying with me tomorrow, I want to help you get ready. You better bring that dress." she said, winking at me as she downed her pint.

"Right won't be long, I need the loo, no flirting whilst I'm gone." Sandra said, moving the table slightly to let herself out. I shook my head laughing. I took my phone from my pocket and started scrolling, checking up on social media when out of nowhere I heard loads of glasses smash. I looked up and saw Jack racing to the bar, I stood up trying to see what was going on.

"It's alright I've got you." I heard Jack shout as he disappeared in front of the bar. I walked around to see if I could help and was shocked to see Sandra collapsed at the bottom. My heart sank.

"Sandra! Sandra!" I said, in a panic.

"I'm alright, I just felt a bit dizzy, too much beer." she said, trying to get herself up from the floor.

"There you go, drink that." Jack gave her a glass of water.

"She's alright." Jack said to me, hugging me from behind. I had never been so worried. As soon as Sandra had finished her water, I helped her up, me on one arm, Jack on the other and I gave her the biggest hug.

"Hey don't worry."

"Are you sure you're alright?" Sandra pulled away from me and held my face in her hands.

"Listen to me, I am always here okay? Always." she wrapped her arms around me again.

"Sorry about the glasses." I heard her say to Jack.

"No worries." Jack put his hand on Sandra's shoulders before starting to clear up all of the broken glass. I held on to her.

My shift the next day was a little awkward, I had told Amy that I was going to Megan's birthday party when she asked me if I had any plans for the weekend. I didn't even think about how everyone would react. I think some of them were a little jealous because they had been working at the salon for so long and didn't get an invite. I honestly think that I was just in the right place at the right time. I don't think Megan would have even thought twice about inviting me if I wasn't working when she had her meltdown. I didn't go on about it on my shift, I tried to go out of my way to get the staff anything they needed, make them coffee, help them clean down and set up their work stations, they weren't nasty to me or anything, there was just some jealous tension. I wasn't worried about it though, I had bigger things to worry about.

I really couldn't wait to leave work that day and make my way over to Sandra's to get ready. I decided to listen to Sandra and wear the red ball gown dress, I did want to make a statement, and I did want to arrive in style. So I thought what harm can it do?

Vanessa was at work that day, I heard her a few times on the phone but I didn't see her. I knew I would see her at the party though and that made me feel very nervous. Once my shift had finished, I headed into the shopping centre to pick up a present for Megan. I remember by that point, I was very content and stable financially. I was still living in my bedsit but it was definitely my home. I had made it a home, it looked great, stylish, full of personality, you wouldn't recognise it from when I first moved in. I was earning good money from the salon and still getting some government help, the bedsit was cheap so I did manage to save a lot. And of course I still had some money left from Sandra, so I was doing well.

I had no idea what to get Megan, I didn't even know her, I had only met her twice. I figured she would already have most things anyway so I went down the sentimental route. I decided to get her something that would mean something to her. I went to a small designer boutique not too far away from the salon called Oceans to have a browse. I had never been in it before but obviously I had seen it when walking to and from work. It was only small, the building was painted a deep blue colour with the word 'OCEAN' in black, hanging from the top. There were huge windows at either side of the entrance. In each window held glass display cabinets of the most beautiful handbags, shoes and sunglasses.

When I went inside, the colours were the same as the outside, black and deep blue. There was a large glass display table in the middle of the store, full of sunglasses all neatly placed. I noticed shelving surrounding the walls with more luxury items. The till area was to the back of the shop, and when I made my way closer to it, I noticed all of the jewellery that was on display in glass boxes under the unit, all catching the light perfectly, enhancing their crystals and diamonds.

"May I help you." a very smartly dressed man called Liam said from behind the till.

"Yes I am looking for a gift for someone's birthday tonight."

"What kind of thing were you looking for?"

"I have no idea, something sentimental?" I said, looking around in awe of all the beautiful items.

"May I?" Liam suggested that I look at something in more detail. He took a key from his pocket and leant down to open one of the glass boxes underneath containing some of the jewellery. I waited with excitement with what he was about to show me. He stood up and placed a sterling silver necklace with two interlocking hearts on a glass plate, the plate reflected the silver sparkles to perfection. "This is the symbol of friendship." he said, with passion about the product.

"Wow." I said, moving my hand over the heart shapes at the centre of the necklace.

"What is the price of this?"

"This retails at £599.00."

Bloody hell I thought? I could afford it but it was a very expensive gift to get someone that you barely knew. Plus it was way more than I actually wanted to spend. I didn't want to sound cheap though.

"It is a little out of my price range if I am honest." Liam nodded.

"We do have this in a bracelet too, it actually went on sale today, would you like me to show you that?"

"Yes please."

Liam put the necklace away and took out a long golden box with a black and blue ribbon tied around it. He gently pulled the ribbon and held the box to me before slowly opening it up in front of me. Inside was the sparkliest, sterling silver bracelet full of small diamonds. In the centre were the two interlocking hearts, I absolutely loved it, it looked really elegant and classy.

"We only have a few of these left, I could do this for £299.00." he said, still with the same passion. It was still way more than I wanted to spend, but I did want to get Megan something that meant something, that was meaningful and that didn't look cheap. I didn't have that much time to get anything so I decided to take it.

"Yes I will have it, could I have it gift-bagged and tagged too please."

"Yes of course." I watched as Liam put the golden box in one of the Oceans small designer black gift bags, he handed me a card, envelope and pen so I could write something to go with the gift. I thought about what to say for a few minutes.

The chat meant a lot to me. Thank you.
Happy Birthday, Love Zoe x

"Thanks so much." I said to Liam as I paid with my credit card and rushed to leave. The next stop was Sandra's!

When I arrived at Sandra's I was surprised to see Jack there. Sandra had invited him round so he could see me in the red dress, of course she did. She was so keen on me and Jack becoming a couple, she was determined to be my fairy godmother. I didn't mind and it was actually really good fun. There was music playing, we were drinking beer, all while Sandra did my hair and makeup and Jack flirted his little way around me. I spent the entire time getting ready just laughing with the people that meant the world to me. I couldn't wait to show them what I had bought, they both really liked it but both had a reaction when I told them how much it actually cost.

"Bloody hell Zoe, I hope she appreciates it." Sandra said, whilst holding the bracelet up to the light to see all the diamonds sparkle. Sandra was actually very good at hair and makeup, by that point my hair was a little bit longer than a bob, it was more shoulder length, still blonde, and I still wore it straight. Not that night though, Sandra waved all my hair to make it look like it did naturally, feeling the waves drop down my back made me feel like me again. My hair was part of my identity and when I changed my appearance I definitely lost a little bit of that. Jack loved it and kept telling me how beautiful I was. My makeup was pretty natural, some foundation- blusher- highlighter, with black smokey eyes and nude lips. Then the moment came that everyone was waiting for, well Sandra and Jack...the red dress.

I went upstairs with Sandra who helped me put the dress on, it felt just as amazing to be in the dress as it did the first time. I remember looking at myself in her bedroom mirror and just being speechless again, both of us were. The emotions came right back to us as she smiled at me through the mirror. Jack couldn't wait to see me, he kept shouting up the stairs to hurry us up.

"Come on! How much longer?" Jack kept saying. We found it hilarious.

Standing overwhelmed at the top of the stairs I saw that Jack was waiting at the bottom, there was a moment of silence as we looked at each other in the eyes and shared a warm smile. I always imagined what it must have been like to attend a prom or something, and I felt in that moment it was pretty close to that magical feeling. I really did feel like the most beautiful girl in the world. Before long the taxi was beeping for me outside, I rushed to do my final checks before saying goodbye to Sandra and Jack. I took a deep breath and stepped outside, I was heading to Megan's.

Chapter 12
A Whole New World

Arriving at Megan's house was like arriving at a movie premier, it was out of this world. The taxi drove down a long hidden drive surrounded by trees and flowers. There was a small water fountain in the centre of the open drive where the house stood behind. I saw posh, expensive looking cars being parked in random places or dropping people off, two Lamborghinis, 3 Porsches to name but a few. I felt a little embarrassed that I was showing up in a local taxi. The house itself was stunning, a grand looking three floor, cladded house stood neatly, partly covered in the greenest ivy. The paintwork of the house was grey and black and done to perfection, hanging baskets were placed neatly around the whole house covered in the biggest silver and pink balloons I had ever seen. Large plants stood by the main entrance door covered in the sparkliest lights. I could see people gathered, all dressed up in their fanciest clothes, hugging and kissing each. There was so much going on.

I got out of the taxi and looked around wondering where to go. I didn't recognise anyone, not that I had expected to, but I was hoping someone would approach me so I could tag along with them. But everyone just kept to their own groups, it was very cliquey. I started to walk around the fountain, taking the sight in, it really was just beautiful. It felt like a whole new world away from my bedsit back in the city centre. I felt a whole world away from the girl I was when I arrived at my bedsit, none of it felt real, I suppose in a way it wasn't. I listened to the sounds of the flowing water the fountain was making and looked up to the sky, feeling a sense of calm. I had no idea what to expect, but I was there now so I was just going to try and enjoy myself. After a while I was startled by a group of people laughing loudly, they were making their way out of sight around the side of the house, so I decided to follow them. I walked for what seemed like a long time through a cobbled alley to the back of the house, where I soon realised the party was taking place.

A huge white gazebo could be seen at the back of the garden covered in balloons, there were flashing lights coming from inside of it and music could be heard. I saw children running around on the grass, playing, having fun, dressed up in their little suits and party dresses. People were gathered with champagne flutes chatting away while servers, dressed in black were carrying trays of more champagne and nibbles. It was getting busier with more people coming from all directions. Opposite the gazebo at the other end of the garden were two patio doors, they were held open with massive *'happy birthday'* balloon decorations, they were a silver colour and I remember how dazzling they looked with all the different lights reflecting off them. I could see the grand looking kitchen that stood inside the house, it was so sparkly, all white and silver, bottles of champagne could be seen on every work unit. It took my breath away.

"You alright love?" I heard from behind me. I turned around and a smartly dressed man stood in front of me, holding a pile of gifts all neatly wrapped with pale pink bows on each one.

"I'm not sure where to go, Megan invited me." I said, a little nervous and feeling very out of place.

"Hang on, are you Zoe?" he said, with a huge smile on his face. I nodded.

"Megan's told me all about you, come with me love. I'm Daniel by the way."

"Hi Daniel." I followed him into the house where he put all the presents he was carrying on one of the kitchen units. He walked me through the kitchen into the open plan living room which was all decorated in white and silver flock wallpaper. A huge chandelier hung in the middle of the ceiling, cream leather sofas made an 'L' shape in the centre of the room, white shaggy rugs dotted around the white marbled floor. Abstract paintwork hung on the high walls, I didn't know where to look, there was an open fireplace with logs placed around the edges, it was burning softly letting out just enough heat to feel.

"Wait here, I'll let Megan know you've arrived." I stood by the window which was draped in silk curtains and looked out onto the front drive with the water fountain, everything was so perfect. I remember thinking how lucky Megan was. How did she get so lucky in life? And I didn't? It didn't seem fair.

"Zoe!" Megan came rushing towards me, she gave me a huge hug.

"I'm so glad you came."

"You look amazing!" I responded in absolute awe of her. Her dress was black and fitted tightly to her body, it had a small trail at the end and was completely backless. Her hair was all wavy with a diamond encrusted headband, you could just about see her pearl earrings which complimented her pearl necklace hung from her neck. Obviously her makeup was glowing.

"This is for you." I gave her the small gift bag containing the gift I got her.

"Awe you didn't need to bother, bless you." Megan took the bag and opened it in front of me. I stood watching nervously hoping she would like it, she was silent for a while when she saw what I had bought her.

"Zoe, it's beautiful, thank you so much." She put the bracelet on and kissed my cheek, holding my hand to follow her.

"Come help me finish getting ready." It was just utter madness.

I stood with all Megan's friends and family in front of the gazebo at the back of the house. Everyone had a glass of something to toast Megan's arrival. There must have been a good few hundred people there. I didn't even know ten people, there was no way I could ever have a birthday party like that one. It was nice having 1-1 time with Megan beforehand, we didn't do much: topped up our make-up, took a few selfies, she added me on social media and I accepted, it was just fun. But finding myself stood amongst everyone, I did feel nervous. I did get some looks from people wondering who I was, but they never came over to ask and I was too nervous to start any type of conversations. These were the high class people of society, I didn't want to ruin my first impressions with anyone, so I kept to myself.

We all stood waiting for Megan to arrive so we could sing 'happy birthday' to her. It didn't take me long to realise that someone was staring at me. I could feel their intense dagger out of the corner of my eye. I tried to ignore it but whoever was looking at me was persistent. I didn't want to look, I tried so hard to ignore the uneasy feeling I was getting. When I did eventually turn around it was Vanessa! My heart sunk, she made sure I saw her and then she turned away from me talking to the people around her. I couldn't hear what she was saying but I figured she was talking about me because all the people around her looked at me too. I smiled to be polite and then I casually turned away.

Vanessa definitely stood out that night, of course she looked amazing, she always did. Her outfit was the loudest there, literally. A golden shimmery flowy dress that touched the floor, caught every single light. Her hair was curled to perfection and her necklace was blinding, shiny crystal drops hung all around her neck. I remember wanting to look over at her again but everyone started singing. Megan could be seen with Daniel walking towards the patio doors, hand in hand with huge smiles on their faces. We all sung and applauded Megan who then took a microphone off the DJ doing all the music from near the gazebo.

"Thank you all so much for coming, it really does mean the world to share my birthday with all my wonderful friends and family. I also want to welcome Zoe..."

I shit myself! What? Me? Why? I stood like a rabbit caught in headlights.

"I haven't known Zoe for long, in fact we met only weeks ago properly at Vanessa's salon but she is the most incredible girl. She got me this beautiful gift for my birthday and I would love for you to all get to know her and make her feel welcome." I was in shock staring at Megan who just kept smiling and winking at me. Everyone clapped and all of a sudden music came on and I was swamped with people. All wanting to know who I was? What I did for a living? Where did I come from? It was chaos, I felt famous. I had never had so much attention before. I didn't really like it.

"Zoe, darling." Vanessa made her way through the crowd and kissed me, cheek by cheek.

"You look incredible." she said.

I didn't know what to say to her but I was very overwhelmed and so I decided to play along.

"Thank you, so do you."

"I need a word with my employee." she said to everyone who was eager to get to know me.

"Always working, she never bloody stops." a guy said from behind. In fact it was the same guy who she was with on her birthday. Remember I told you about when she got drunk? The fancy bar I followed her to? And the silver car had to come and pick them up? I had seen him a few times by that point. But I still wasn't sure who he was but it wasn't really relevant at the time.

Vanessa took my arm and led me through the crowds of people inside the house where we sat in the kitchen. There was a small black sofa hidden to the left of the room, a glass oval coffee table placed in front. I noticed all the baby toys that were neatly put away in colourful storage cubes. A pink fluffy rabbit doll caught my attention, sat neatly on top of one of the cubes, it's black eyes staring straight at me.

It was silent for a while.

"You've made quite the impression on Megan haven't you?" Vanessa said, as we both sat down next to each other on the sofa. I knew what she was doing, she was trying to intimidate me.

"She's really nice." I said, a little unsure of where the conversation was actually going. The last time we had spoken properly was in her office and it was extremely intense, where I walked out on her after telling her a few home truths. I suppose I had to remember that she was still my boss... amongst other things...and I didn't actually want her to hate me. Having said that she was impossible to read and I was clearly getting under her skin.

"What are you up to Zoe?" she asked, looking at me directly in the eyes. Vanessa threw me, I wasn't expecting her to ask that.

"I'm not up to anything, Megan invited me, I'm just wanting to have a nice night."

"I don't know Zoe, there is something about you. I just can't put my finger on it."

I shrugged and looked over to the rabbit teddy, focusing on it's jet black, button eyes.

"Guys come on! The party's outside." Daniel interrupted our chat when he came into the kitchen to get another bottle of champagne. I quickly got up and left Vanessa sitting on the sofa.

Was she onto me? I really wasn't sure.

I had an amazing time at Megan's birthday, I felt so lucky to have been invited and part of her special day. I did feel like I didn't belong there at first, but as the evening went on and I engaged with more people, I relaxed into myself and had a really good night. I even got up and danced with everyone at one point. I realised that we weren't actually that different. I mean lifestyles- YES- but we were all just people, some with more money than others.

I remember towards the end of the night, it got much quieter, people were slowly starting to go home. It must have been around midnight because I remember hearing a lady say to who she was with "bloody hell it's midnight, we better get going soon." I decided it was probably the right time for me to go too. I phoned a taxi who said they would pick me up in about 45 minutes because they were really busy. A few of the other guests said they would drop me off, but I didn't want to put them out and if I'm completely honest, see where I lived.

"I could do with going to the bathroom before I leave." I said, to one of the other guests.

"It's straight up the stairs, the door directly in front of you." One of the ladies replied whilst checking her bag, making sure she had everything before she left.

"Awe thank you, nice to meet you." I headed for the bathroom.

"You too love."

There were still people gathered in the gazebo, gathered in the garden, I noticed a few children fast asleep on the garden sofa swing. When I walked through the patio into the kitchen, I saw Megan and Daniel kissing, they looked so happy, so content. It was nice to see, I didn't disturb them, I carried on through the living room to find the staircase. I admired the beautifully decorated living room again as I made my way through to the glass sliding doors to the main entrance of the house. The first thing I noticed was the glass circular table holding the most beautiful, biggest bouquet of pink roses. It was situated perfectly in the middle of the front door and the bottom of the staircase. The floor was pure white, sparkly marble, crisp clean. The staircase was like something out of a film, the stairs got bigger until you reached the top, cream carpeted and white bannister. I took my shoes off and remembered how soft the carpet felt on my feet, it was just magical. I felt like Cinderella.

I made my way to the top of the staircase, gently touching the bannister with my hand as I did, it was like walking on a cloud. When I got to the top I saw the bathroom straight away, the door was left slightly ajar and I could see the free standing, silver footed bath in the centre of the room. I should have gone straight in and out, but I couldn't help myself, my eyes were wandering everywhere. I had never been in such a beautiful place before, I was in awe. The carpet was just as soft on the landing, it was huge upstairs, a big rectangle space with dazzling, silver painted doors everywhere, I noticed a few abstract looking items neatly placed in areas of the floor space. A large green plant almost touching the ceiling in a black plant pot, a white horse head, possibly made of marble and a stack of brown, vintage looking suitcases that acted as shelves. I looked down to the bottom of the stairs, there was no one in sight, so I decided to have a look around. I carefully walked over to one of the doors which had a beautiful handmade plaque on it saying *'dreams don't work unless you do.'* I took a moment staring at the carefully thought out words, before holding down the door handle and slowly pushing it open. I felt guilty snooping but I couldn't help myself, I was curious beyond belief.

The room was dark but I soon found a light switch on the left hand side of the wall. It was a room full of Megan's things, all her designer clothes hung on rails around the outside of the room. Directly in front of me on the pure white wall was a canvas of Megan when she was pregnant with Chloe, I remember her smile stretching over the entire canvas, she looked so happy. I could see designer shoes dotted around the room, a pair of Louboutins caught my attention by a tall free standing mirror in the corner of the room. It was like Megan's sanctuary, her safe space away from the rest of the world. There was a white circular table in the centre of the room, full of folders, papers and books. I walked over and took a closer look. It looked like Megan was studying or planning to study Interior Design, she had post- it notes dotted around of when she could start certain courses. Megan clearly had more ambitions than just being a mum, she was clearly very ambitious and although it seemed like she had everything she could have ever wished for, she still wanted more and to better herself. What I would have given to be more like her. I was suddenly startled by some laughter I could hear outside and so I rushed to turn the light off and shut the door quickly behind me. I shouldn't have even been in there, I was terrified of getting caught.

As I rushed to the bathroom I could hear someone saying "Mummy. Mummy." I stopped on the landing and looked over my shoulder to where the sound was coming from. Another hand painted plaque could be seen, this time in big white and pink letters it said 'CHLOE' I really wasn't sure what to do. Do I go and get Megan? Do I shout down the stairs? Do I ignore her? I couldn't just leave her, it didn't feel right so I made my way to her bedroom.

The room was dark, fairy lights everywhere, showing certain areas of her room. A big dolls house just under the window to the right of the room, a rocking horse to the left. It was a beautiful, pink, girly room, perfect for any princess. How lucky was this little girl I remember thinking. There was a princess-shaped bed in the middle of the room, with a pink canopy hanging over the top. I followed the shape of the canopy with my eyes all the way down to the bed and there she was, there was Chloe. This little, tiny girl sat up in her animal print pjs, her brown wavy hair a mess from where she had slept on it, she was rubbing her eyes, still asking for her mum. I was about to walk over to her, to comfort her, when I felt someone grab my shoulder.

125

"What on earth do you think you're doing?" It was Vanessa.

"She was asking for her mum, I was on the way to the bathroom, I just wanted to..."

"Yes, alright. Well I'm here now so... hello my darling." Vanessa brushed past me and sat on the bed, moving Chloe's hair out of her face. I quietly left the room, glancing back at Chloe before I did. I knew at that moment that something wasn't right with Vanessa, it was like she was scared of me getting closer to her family, closer to Chloe.

It was a good night though, one of the best nights I had ever had. For the first time I felt like I was someone in the world, like I belonged in society, I had a part to play too. I met some really nice people and got even closer to Megan, finally feeling like I had a friend in her. I didn't know it at the time, but what happened that night would go on to change the direction of my entire future.

Chapter 13
Heartbreak

The start of a fresh week, I felt a different kind of energy about me, a more confident version of myself since that weekend at Megan's. If I really wanted to then I could be 'one of those people' 'the elite'. I was more than capable of it and that to me was powerful. I could train myself to be whoever I wanted to be and that was how I was going to get to the truth.

When I arrived at work, it looked very different. It had been transformed into a meeting room, there was a large projector towards the back of the salon and the lounge area for the clients was full of booklets. I said hello to everyone and took a seat where I could find space, waiting for the meeting to start. This was my first proper meeting with the company, so I was a little nervous and wasn't really sure what to expect. I saw Vanessa rushing around whilst speaking to a supplier on the phone. A few potential clients walked in but other staff members had to tell them we were shut for the morning. I sat peacefully observing my surroundings.

At around 10am, Vanessa could be heard telling us all to take a seat, she stood in front of us all with a tiny remote to operate the projector.

"Thank you everyone for taking the time to come in this morning, I know some of you are off today, so thank you. A lot of you have been to these meetings before, but there are a few newbies here, so these meetings are really just an update on what's been happening, where we are thriving to go etc. etc. and of course there is the option for your feedback too..." Vanessa said, going on and on about the importance of teamwork, goals, ambition, striving to be better than the best in the business, she loved the sound of her own voice, or so it seemed.
We were given booklets about the salon's success last year, teamwork question sheets that we had to fill out and then there was a group discussion. One of the questions was:

How can I go above what is required of me as a stylist?

Another one,
What can I do to help motivate my co-workers?

Some were more detailed than others but it did work in getting us all to engage in a conversation.

"I would also like to congratulate Zoe on passing her probation period." Vanessa said, applauding me, everyone else joined in. I was surprised she had made a public matter of it. I wasn't even sure if she would want me to carry on working for her, she clearly didn't like me, it certainly felt that way. But I wasn't going to walk away from a job that I actually loved.

"Thank you so much." I said, a little taken back.

"Don't thank me. Thank everyone around you, you have clearly made an impression on them too." Vanessa looked me dead in the eye, she really couldn't help herself, every positive thing she said to me came with a backhanded comment. I was getting used to her by now.

Vanessa then played us a video.

"Here comes the video, she plays this every time." one of the old members of staff whispered. He noticed me looking at him and smiled, I smiled back and looked curiously at the video that started to play. It was a video about the salon since Vanessa took over, lots of facts and figures thrown at us. I won't lie, I was very impressed, she was very successful and I admired that about her. The salon was actually Vanessa's mothers who named the salon after her once she was born, it had been in her family for generations. Before Vanessa's mum made it into a hair salon, it was actually a boutique shoe shop owned by Vanessa's grandmother. The video seemed to go on for ages, I could see some of the staff yawning and stretching, longing for it to finish, eventually it did.

"Thank you everyone, if you could make this look like a salon again I'd appreciate that. Zoe, a word please." Vanessa said, before ushering me to her office.

Why me? I thought as I followed her, she told me to take a seat as she held the door open for me, I heard her close the door behind me. I couldn't help it, no matter how confident I had started to become, when I was around Vanessa I felt scared. I guess because of who I thought she was, because of the truth. Vanessa rustled around her desk and handed me a white A4 envelope. I took it with anticipation and looked inside of it before taking it out and holding it in front of me.

I paused in shock. I just couldn't believe it. I could feel my eyes watering. Vanessa had given me a full time contract at the salon.

"You deserve it." Vanessa said, offering me a tissue.

"I don't know what to say."

"You don't need to say anything, you've proven yourself to me."

"I thought you hated me."

"Well you know what they say. Keep your friends close but your enemies closer...just kidding." Vanessa said, kicking back on her chair.

"Just don't let me down." I took some tissue and wiped under my eyes. Before I could answer her office door swung open and Megan walked in, Chloe giggling away in the pram.

"Awe sorry, I didn't know you were in a meeting." Megan said, looking flustered.

"No, don't worry about it."Vanessa rushed to help Megan with the pram. I stood up.

"Hey Zoe you alright?"

"Yeah I'm good, thanks." I said, smiling at Megan and glancing over at Vanessa who was now holding Chloe. Chloe looked at me and she just kept smiling. I didn't see her properly that night at Megan's but she really was beautiful, she looked like a doll.

"Awe you smiling at Zoe." Megan said, holding onto Chloe's hand.

"I should get back to work, thank you so much again Vanessa." I said.

"What's this?" Megan asked intrigued, she could tell I had been crying.

"Zoe will be working for the salon full time starting next week."

"That's amazing! Well done love." Megan rushed over to hug me.

"We need to celebrate, why don't you come over for dinner next Friday?"

"Oh..." I didn't know what to say.

"Please it's just family, I would love to celebrate with you." I don't know why but I looked over to Vanessa for approval. I didn't want to sabotage the full time job I had just been given.

"I think that sounds like a great idea." Vanessa said, winking at me. I took a deep breath and headed back to work, holding onto that contract like my life depended on it. That was my future, or so I hoped. I remember at that moment feeling like everything was starting to make sense, things were starting to fall into place, and it felt amazing. I had come a long way since my first day in that bedsit. I had achieved more in those months at the salon than I ever did in the eighteen years before that. It was difficult though, sometimes I felt like a fraudster, I didn't get success being me, the real me. I had pretended to be someone else for so long, I didn't really know who I was. I just knew I needed the truth, that would be the greatest success of all.

When I left work I arranged to meet Jack at The Plant Pot to tell him my news. I was so excited walking into the bar with my contract in my bag. Jack was standing behind the bar when I arrived with a huge grin on his face, just like he always had whenever he saw me. I waved my contract up and down, and he met me at the end of the bar.

"Hello you." he said, leaning on to the bar with all his weight, his massive tattooed arms looking absolutely gorgeous.

"So you are now looking at a full time member of staff at Vanessa's Hair and Beauty salon!" I said, barely able to contain myself.

"That's amazing news!" Jack said, before leaning in for a kiss. He pulled away quickly when he realised what he had done.

"I'm so sorry..."

"No, don't be." I said, looking at him. I took a moment because I really didn't have any experience with boys.

"I really like you Jack." I leaned over the bar and kissed him back, he held my face with his hands before pulling away to look at me, he looked me in the eyes and kissed my forehead before hugging me tight.
"Let me get you a drink."

Fire. That's how I felt. My entire body had never felt so alive. I was in a bubble, nothing else mattered, nothing.

"Have you told Sandra yet?" Jack said, passing me a glass of champagne.
"No I'll ring her in a bit, champagne hey."
"Anything for my girl." He said, laughing.
"Yep okay, that was cheesy." I took a sip of my drink, feeling the happiest I had ever felt. Jack had to serve some other customers so I took a seat at the bar and read over my contract properly. It was life changing for me, full time hours, a good salary, a career. I could move out of my bedsit into a proper apartment, I could travel if I wanted to, I was in control of my life, anything was possible.

That day should have been one of the happiest days of my entire life but it ended up being one of the worst. I waited around half an hour before I took my phone out of my bag to ring Sandra, I couldn't wait to tell her my news, she was going to be so happy for me. I would never have even got that far if it wasn't for Sandra. I owed Sandra my life.

ZOE:

"Hi, it's me, I've got some news. Ring me when you can."

I left Sandra a voicemail and then carried on talking to Jack. He made sure my champagne glass was never empty and did everything he could do to celebrate with me. The bar did get more and more busier with students and a few birthday gatherings and so I grabbed a seat in the window away from all the hustle and bustle. I tried Sandra again but it went straight to voicemail, it wasn't like her not to answer. I never heard from her after Megan's birthday party either, which was unusual because she was always wanting to know all the details. I was getting worried so I tried again and again and again...until.

MAN:

"Hello, who is this?" an abrupt man said down the phone to me.

ZOE:

"Hello...Hi...my name is Zoe. I'm trying to get hold of Sandra." I said, surprised and confused. No one answered, there was a lot of silence.

ZOE:

"Hello, hello, is there anybody there?" I was getting spooked.

MAN:

"Sandra's dead." The man hung up, all I could hear was the dial tone.

I couldn't move. I was numb. Was this a dream? A really bad dream? I didn't know what to do. I couldn't see properly, my eyes felt puffy and my cheeks were soaked with tears. I needed to leave, I felt like I couldn't breathe. Everything was a blur, all my eyes could see were different colours, some brighter than others as I managed to make my way home. I won't ever forget that night. I collapsed on my bed and sobbed, I couldn't stop myself. I had never felt pain like it. It couldn't be true, it couldn't be. I rushed up and grabbed my phone, I had messages and missed calls from Jack but all I wanted was Sandra. I held the phone to my ear and sat on the end of my bed, it rang for some time.

MAN:
"Hello." It was the same man from before.
ZOE:
"Hi, please don't hang up on me, please." I said, sobbing, crying down the phone like the heartbroken mess I was. "I don't understand, she can't be."
MAN:
"I'm sorry, I found her last night."
ZOE:
"Who are you?" I asked, longing for answers.
MAN:
"I'm her son."
ZOE:

"I didn't think you were close any more?" I was getting frustrated because I didn't understand. Sandra had always told me that she wasn't close to her son.

MAN:

"We spoke everyday, I tried to get home to see her whenever I could since the illness."

ZOE:

"Hang on, what illness?"

MAN:

"Mum had cancer."

I dropped the phone, running to the bathroom, to throw my guts up. None of this made any sense, how could Sandra be dead. It wasn't possible. I tried to gather myself together to go back to the phone.

ZOE:

"Are you still there?"

MAN:

"Yes."

ZOE:

"I don't understand. I was only with her at the weekend, she was fine."

MAN:

"I never got a look in since you came along, she was obsessed with you. Look, I need to go. I'm sorry."

ZOE:

"No...Please! Hello? Hello?" There was no one there. The line went quiet.

What the actual fuck just happened?! I stood in the middle of my bedsit, clutching onto my phone, tears running down my face feeling like I had a lost part of me. I was in complete shock, I didn't want to believe it, I needed Sandra, I needed her.

Chapter 14
Reality Check

    I was so cold. I couldn't feel my body but I could hear it, rumbling away to itself. It was the worst feeling in the world. I was there for two days, lying on my bedsit floor, not being able to face what had happened. How could I carry on? Nothing made sense, not without Sandra in my life. I just had no idea how to deal with it. I lifted my head from the floor and felt like I had the worst hangover known, the tension was unbelievable. I stood over the bathroom sink and washed my face with cold water. The ice cold water felt amazing drenching my burnt out face. I looked at my reflection in the mirror, my makeup from two days before could still be seen but incredibly smudged around my eyes where I had been crying. My hair was tangled and dry looking, I looked so pale and unwell. I took a glass from the bathroom cabinet and filled it with cold water which I drank in one go before slowly returning to the main area of my bedsit, holding onto the wall for support as I did.

    I found my phone on the kitchen table, it had no battery life and was completely dead. Probably not the best word to use under those circumstances but you know what I mean. I plugged it in the kitchen and left it alone whilst I went to open the main window to let in some much needed air, the atmosphere felt stale and stuffy. I had no sense of real time at that moment, I was completely disoriented. I didn't really have a plan but I knew that I couldn't just sit and stay in the rut that I had started to be in. I went into the bathroom and turned on the shower ready to indulge in it, when out of nowhere my phone started buzzing non-stop. I thought it was going to explode. I had so many missed calls and messages from Jack and Vanessa. Jack asking *'how I was?'* Vanessa asking *'where I was?'* then I remembered the promotion and needing to go into work. I'd missed two whole days without warning, Vanessa would never understand, well I didn't think she would. In her eyes I had just gone AWOL. I felt like I was probably already fired. It was all too good to be true anyway. How could someone like me ever get a promotion at the best hair salon in Manchester? I wasn't that lucky.

I was still scrolling through all the messages I had missed:

JACK: Please call me back x
JACK: Babe, what's wrong?
JACK: Will you please talk to me? I am worried about you! X
VANESSA: You are 30 minutes late. This is not a great start considering your recent promotion.
VANESSA: Zoe. Where are you? I am very disappointed in you.

VANESSA: Shall I look for someone else Zoe? I should not be running around after you, contact me immediately.

They went on and on and on... all of a sudden the phone rang whilst in my hand, it was Vanessa. I froze, it was like she knew that I had my phone, it kept ringing and ringing, she wasn't giving up.

ZOE:
"Hello." I finally answered.
VANESSA:
"Where have you been? In fact do not even bother to answer that. You get yourself into work in the next half an hour young lady or else."

Before I had the chance to say anything, Vanessa hung up. I realised I couldn't just hide away, I needed to face the world. It was a struggle but I got myself ready for work. I felt guilty for even choosing an outfit to wear, for doing my makeup, my hair. How could life just go on? How could life be so normal outside of these walls? My life had just been blown apart. I felt sick to the stomach as I made my way into work. I just knew there was going to be no reasoning with Vanessa. I didn't have it in me to argue or to be yelled at, I didn't have the energy. Vanessa had said on the phone I had half an hour to get into work. I was well over an hour by the time I had got ready and walked to the salon.

When I arrived you could feel the tension, no one really spoke or looked at me, clearly they were all talking about me and my whereabouts. I headed straight to Vanessa's office where I knocked quietly before opening the door. When I walked in, Vanessa was sitting behind her desk on her phone, when she saw me she slammed her phone down on the table with rage.

"Sit down now." she said, looking furious. I did what she asked because like I said, I didn't have it in me to fight with her.

"What do you think you're playing at?"

"Vanessa." I quietly said.

"No Zoe. After everything, I didn't think you would let me down so quickly. Do you think I hand out promotions left, right and centre? Because I can assure you, I don't.

"Vanessa." I quietly repeated.

"You had an amazing opportunity here to actually make something of yourself. I took a chance on you Zoe, you know that don't you? I mean who wouldn't want to be part of this world that I have created?!"

There was no shutting her up. It was like I had triggered something inside of her, she couldn't stop herself, all this hatred just came out.

"You really are a silly young girl. I don't want someone like you in my team..."

"She's dead." I said, almost complacent, not even sure if she would hear me.

"She's dead." I repeated, the words almost piercing my tongue. My guts tensing in pain, my eyes blistering with redness from trying to hold back all the tears that I knew would never stop once I started. I just couldn't believe I was saying it.

"Sandra is dead." I said, for the third time before getting up and heading to the door to leave.

"Zoe." Vanessa rushed up to me and stood in front of the door.

"No you're not going." she said, holding onto my arms. I struggled with her a bit because I just wanted to leave. I felt weak, vulnerable and like I couldn't breathe properly.

"I don't know what I'm meant to do." I yelled. "How do I deal with this?"

"Come here, it's alright." Vanessa held me whilst I sobbed my heart out for Sandra.

"I'm so sorry Zoe, I shouldn't have spoken to you like that. I had no idea. You're safe with me darling." She held me tight and didn't let me go until I pulled away.

That moment was a pivotal moment in my story. It was a moment I had been longing for. I felt safe, secure, important, wanted- loved even. I felt like I could trust her, but I was wrong. I was so very wrong.

I watched Vanessa hold my hand trying to comfort me. I had so many moments like that with Vanessa, it was always so dramatic and emotional. One extreme to the other. But it never seemed to last long or go anywhere. Vanessa would hold me, support me then in the next breath she would be distant and cold with me, a lot of the time unapproachable. I hoped that now it would be different. Her hand was tight around mine as we both sat on the lounge sofa in her office. Her bright red nails were all I could see whilst she clasped my hand tight through my red, watery eyes.

"For what it's worth, what I said before, I shouldn't have." Vanessa said, with what seemed like genuine remorse.

"It doesn't matter." my voice was small.

"I'm not good with things like this. I never have been." Vanessa said, trying to justify her words.

"You're good around Chloe." I said, almost blaise and not really knowing what I was saying or where the conversation was leading.

"I'm not maternal, not naturally." she gave my hand a tight squeeze.

"You have a son and Megan though."

"Yes and I wouldn't change them but..." Vanessa hesitated.

"But what?"

Vanessa let go of my hand, she seemed hot and bothered, like she almost said something she shouldn't.

"Sandra was all I had." Vanessa nodded.

"Yes. Megan did mention you didn't have any family around. You know Megan thinks a lot of you."

"I like her a lot too."

"How did you meet Sandra?" Vanessa seemed to lose a bit of her confidence when she asked me that.

143

"I've not known her for long, I contacted her to ask for her help with something."

"Help you with what?" Vanessa sat back down next to me, almost too close it made me feel uncomfortable.

"Zoe! Help you with what?" I looked at Vanessa, Vanessa looked at me. It was silent for some time.

"Shit!" My phone went off in my pocket, it made us both jump. I reached for it, it was Jack.

"I really need to answer this." I said, looking at Vanessa for her approval, she nodded reluctantly. I stood up and left Vanessa sitting alone in her office.

ZOE:
"Jack! I am so sorry."
JACK:
"Where have you been? Where are you? Are you alright?" Jack was both relieved that I had finally answered his call and confused about what was going on.
ZOE:
"Jack. I really need to see you."

Jack and I laid in bed at my bedsit. I told him about Sandra and he was in utter shock too, he just couldn't believe it or get his head around it. Sandra had definitely left her mark on both of us, we laid in my bed like two lost puppies looking for their mother, in some ways that wasn't too far from the truth. I laid in Jack's arms, his tight grip

144

around me. Neither of us saying anything but just being there for one another. The only thing I should have been thinking about was Sandra but I couldn't get Vanessa out of my head. There was something about the conversation we had in her office, something didn't feel right. I kept thinking if Jack would have rang just a few minutes later, where would the conversation have gone? What would have been said? Was Vanessa starting to work everything out? Did she have an idea who I could be?

Jack and I definitely got a lot closer since Sandra's death. He was all I really had left in the world, him and finding out the truth about who I was and where I came from.

A week later I got a message from Sandra's son who I found out was called Zack, I was actually with Jack at the time, he was cooking me dinner at my bedsit-hunters chicken and veg. I read the message out loud, me sat at the kitchen table with a beer, Jack stood in the kitchen with a towel over his shoulder, giving me his full attention:

ZACK:
I thought you would want to know, Mum's funeral is at Salford Community Church on Sunday @2pm, short service and burial only.

Those words stuck in my head for the rest of that night.

145

The Friday before Sandra's funeral was Megan's dinner party that I had been invited to. I hadn't been at work much those few weeks leading up to Sandra's funeral. Vanessa said that I could take as much time off as I needed too and do some light PR duties from home, if I wanted to keep busy. I did appreciate her allowing me to do that and so I took her up on the offer. I didn't see Vanessa properly after the chat we had in her office, we mainly communicated through messages and it was always work related. But there was something that she wanted to say, or was trying to get me to say. Something was worrying her and it did really bother me.

I wasn't sure whether or not to cancel the dinner plans. It didn't feel right, going out, enjoying myself, when Sandra was gone. I still had that immense feeling of guilt just doing normal, everyday things but I could almost hear Sandra telling me to *"bloody get on with it girl"*. Megan had messaged me a lot since she found out about Sandra, and it really did mean a lot to me. Having Megan's understanding and support felt amazing. Jack was doing his best to be there for me and I did love spending time with him but no one could replace that mother role that Sandra had started to fill for me. Finding out the truth was now more important than ever! But was I ready?

Chapter 15
Dinner Party

There I was outside Megan's house, standing head to toe in designer clothing, a blue Gujji jumpsuit with black heels and blue ribbon ties. Jack had dropped me off by the water fountain in the front of the drive. It should have brought so much peace and tranquillity, listening to the waterfall, listening to the birds. It was a really calm, beautiful evening, just the gentlest of breezes. But I felt an absolute vulnerable mess inside. I just had one of those feelings, a sickly feeling that I couldn't shake off. And the thought of being in an intimate setting with Vanessa terrified me. I made my way to the grand, silver painted front door, brightly lit with artificial flames at either side. I lifted my hand to the black, lion head, door knocker, when all of a sudden the door swung open.

"Zoe! I am so glad you made it." Megan greeted me a little tipsy with a glass of champagne. She was as warm and welcoming as always, but she already had a lot to drink. "How are you doing?" she asked, kissing me on the cheek and ushering me inside.

"Yeah I'm alright."

"Come through, everyone's in the kitchen." I followed Megan into the kitchen where I immediately saw Vanessa sitting on the sofa with a large glass of red. Her husband, who I found out was called Richard, was sitting with Daniel around the breakfast bar on the island. He was the smartly dressed, white haired guy I had seen with her a few times before. Megan headed straight to the fridge to get another bottle of champagne. I stood and said hello to everyone. "Come and sit next to me." Vanessa said, across the room.

"Don't look so nervous." Richard laughed. I laughed along too but inside I was nervous, apprehensive about what would be brought up. I did want answers- of course I did- but somehow getting closer to the truth in the presence of Vanessa made me question everything. I made my way over to her, she was plumping up the cushions for me to go and sit next to her. Megan followed with a bottle of champagne and an extra glass for me.

"That colour looks beautiful on you." Vanessa said, stroking my hair. I smiled trying not to come across as awkward. Megan gave me a glass of champagne and held her glass in the air.

"To Sandra." Megan said, looking over to me. I thought it was such a nice thing for Megan to do, she didn't know Sandra and had never met her but she knew how much she meant to me.

Daniel and Richard were doing their own thing, talking about football and business, so it was just the three of us sat down putting the worlds to rights. I did relax and ease into the evening the more champagne I drank.

"Are you excited about your promotion?" Megan asked, slurring her words slightly. I nodded.

"I'm looking forward to being more independent, maybe getting my own apartment or something."

"Yes! That would be amazing, invest your money into property, you won't go far wrong." Megan was excited, fully supportive of me. I felt like I knew Megan my whole life, she was so easy to be around.

"It's good to have ambition. I drilled that into you didn't I?" Vanessa said, giving Megan 'the look'.

"You stick with me and I will make sure you don't do anything wrong." Vanessa said, looking back at me, taking over the conversation with her power and authority she seemed to lord over everyone. Megan eventually made herself scarce to sort out the food leaving me alone with Vanessa. I offered to help but of course Megan's reply was... "don't be silly, love, you're our guest."

Vanessa turned to her side of the sofa and pulled up the biggest bottle of red wine I had ever seen. It was almost unbelievable, she filled her glass to the top, watching me as she poured it, she didn't spill a drop. She then put the bottle down and reached for the champagne bottle that was placed in a golden ice bucket on a small coffee table near us. I watched her fill my glass until it was almost overflowing.

"That's enough." I said, worried it would go on Megan's sofa and my dress.

"Do you feel scared around me?" Vanessa asked, putting the champagne back in the bucket. I looked over to Megan who was in her own world, busy, taking things out of the oven and pottering around the kitchen.

"No, I've just got a lot going on." I said, sipping my champagne, avoiding eye contact.

"I just don't think I know the real you Zoe." I went quiet.

Do I just come out and say it? (Actually, yes Vanessa! I think you're my mum. I'm the daughter you left on a doorstep when I was just hours old. Somehow I didn't think that it was appropriate).

"I don't know what you mean?"

"Zoe. One minute you're sassy, confident, gobby and then the next you're acting timid, on edge, scared around me."

"I just don't want to disappoint you." I knew my behaviour was always changing around Vanessa but that's because I never knew how to take her. I tried so hard at the beginning to be someone else, to be more like her. But I wasn't like her, not really and with everything that was going on at the time, the real me was starting to show. Zoe was never confident, sassy, in control, she was vulnerable, shy, weary and emotional and yes she was scared of Vanessa.

"Tell me the truth and you won't disappoint." Vanessa said, edging closer to me on the sofa.

"Truth about what?"

"The other day in my office... What was Sandra helping you do?"

I felt my heart beating in my chest, my hands were starting to stick to my champagne glass. I could feel my cheeks go bright red. I felt like I was getting suffocated by Vanessa's words. I remember thinking if Vanessa was my mum, I would spend the rest of my life in her complete control, just like Megan seemed to be. I took a moment.

"Vanessa... I..."

"Right everyone, dinners ready!" Megan shouted from the kitchen area, looking very pleased with herself. Vanessa grabbed my hand harshly.

"I think you're up to something. This isn't over." Vanessa said, whilst standing up, hovering over me and kissing my forehead, she headed to the dining area and left me sitting wondering what on earth she thought I was plotting. I took a large mouthful of my drink and followed. I had a feeling that things were not going to go to plan. Not at all.

Sitting around the dining table would have been magical if I hadn't had so much going on in my head. Vanessa was making things worse with the constant questions and the way she was around me. I was supposed to be the one ahead of the situation but sometimes I just wasn't sure at all. Megan had gone to so much effort with the interior decorations, it looked so stunning. The circular table sat underneath the most sparkliest chandelier, the silk, grey table cloth complimented the white plates, napkins and marble finish cutlery. It was always so grand and over the top to me but to Megan and her family it was an occasion, and everything was going to be done properly. It was a roast dinner with all the trimmings, served in the middle of the table so everyone could help themselves. It smelt incredible but if I am honest, I felt sick and wasn't really hungry. If anything at that point I was in the mood to get drunk, really really drunk.

The conversation wasn't so intense having Megan, Richard and Daniel there. In fact it flowed pretty well, all of us even laughing at times to jokes that Richard was making. He was a bit of a joker, the total opposite to Vanessa. He was laid back and had a softer approach to life. As the evening went on, I would be lying if I told you that I didn't enjoy it. Drinks were flowing and I became less tense. I could feel myself getting more and more tipsy and I loved it. I needed it. I didn't realise it at the time but things were going to get a whole lot worse.

So, everyone had finished dinner, only bits of food were left on everyone's plate and a little bit of meat left in the centre, most of the veg had gone. Talks were had about who would do the dishes but no one really wanted to get up because like I said, the banter and conversation was flowing. It got to around 9.30pm when Daniel said, "Bloody hell, we better clear this up or they'll still be here in the morning."

"Yeah, with all of us still sitting here." Richard said, laughing, drinking his whisky. Daniel sat next to me and eventually after putting it off for some time, he did stand up to reach across the table to start clearing the plates. As he did, his wallet fell out of his pocket, along with some notes and receipts. It was a black leather wallet- obviously designer. It had a silver logo on it that I couldn't quite make out, not only because of how much I had drunk but because it was too small to read. I reached down to pick it up, not really thinking anything of it. I couldn't help but open the wallet back up to put all his money and receipts in, ready to give it back. Daniel hadn't even noticed, he was busy trying to gather as many plates and cutlery as he could. Holding the wallet in my hand, I started to put everything back together. Then it happened, I saw something. I couldn't believe my eyes. I was in shock, total shock. I couldn't even speak.

Daniel's wallet had a photo section inside, like most do. He had a picture in it, again like most people do. But I recognised the picture. It was a picture of a beautiful young woman in her bathing suit, sitting out in the sun, on some grass, smiling like she had been photographed and wasn't expecting it. It was the same photograph that was left with me as a baby. It was exactly the same.

"Babe you've dropped your wallet." Megan said, shaking her head around to everyone else, noticing that I had it in my hand. Daniel looked over to me and laughed.

153

"Bloody hell, I really do need to get another one, the clasps broken, thanks love." Daniel took it out of my hand, well he tried too, my hands were fixed on the picture. He noticed me staring at it because I heard him say.

"That's Megan, I took that when we were dating, she's still just as beautiful." I let go and he shoved it all back into his back pocket without a care in the world, my hands started to shake. Daniel carried on clearing the table, Richard decided to help. I didn't know what to do, what to say. But someone knew what was going on and someone was watching me. I looked at Megan who was tapping away on her phone, uploading her pictures she took of the evening on social media. When I looked at Vanessa, she looked like she had seen a ghost. In that moment it clicked, everything started to make sense. I got it wrong. I got it so wrong. It wasn't Vanessa who was my mum. It was Megan. And in the same moment I realised it, something happened in Vanessa's head too.

If Megan was my mum, why did she give me up? She had a daughter so she did want children? How did she not recognise me? How did she not feel a connection? Maybe she did? We did get on very well, and she was always supporting me. Was Sandra wrong about Vanessa leaving me that night? Who even is Vanessa? My head was mashed with all the questions I had and alcohol I had drank, I started to feel sick, literally. I couldn't cope with it all, the only person I wanted at that moment was Sandra. And she was gone, I felt so alone. I couldn't even tell Jack because he didn't have a clue what was going on. I think I started to have a panic attack, I got pins and needles in my arms and legs and struggled for breath.

"I think I should take you home." Vanessa said, a little panicked.

"No way, she's not finished her drink yet." Megan said, winking at me, completely oblivious, she was very drunk at that stage.

"It's alright, you ladies just sit there, we'll sort it." Richard said, making an entrance to clear the rest of the plates.

"I thought you would appreciate this." he said, putting down another bottle of champagne in front of us, which Megan jumped up to open.

"I need the bathroom." I must have looked so rude but it was either 'get up and go' or throw up everywhere and have Vanessa put me in her car. I made my way to the top of the stairs to the bathroom, rushing in to lock the door behind me. I threw up almost immediately. All this time I was focusing on Vanessa. All this time I had been getting closer to her without realising the real connection Megan and I had. I needed to speak to Megan without Vanessa knowing, but that was going to be impossible, especially if Vanessa did know who I actually was.

I flushed the toilet and stood over the sink. I looked at my reflection, I looked beautiful but how damaged I was inside. I was so fed up with pretending, of bleaching my hair, all the makeup, expensive clothes that I was terrified of getting dirty. I was just fed up. Part of me wanted to go downstairs and just tell Megan everything, I'd be alright, I'd be safe with everyone there I thought. But then I remembered that I didn't really know these people, I was with strangers. I had no idea what these people were capable of. What would they do to protect each other from the truth? Or to keep the lies? I took some water in the cup of my hand and drank it, trying to settle my head down before heading downstairs, ringing Jack to come and get me and leave as soon as possible. I gathered myself together and unlocked the bathroom door, when I opened it I was shocked to see Vanessa standing there, waiting for me, she put her finger to her mouth.

"Be quiet." she whispered. I was so scared. I looked past her and thought about making a run for it. All of a sudden Vanessa came charging towards me, grabbing my face to keep me quiet. Vanessa locked the door behind us and held me against her, one hand over my mouth so I couldn't scream. I struggled and struggled but she was too strong.

"Zoe stop it." I was physically and emotionally exhausted, so I gave up. I let Vanessa do what she felt like she had to do, she held me in front of the mirror so I could see what was going on.

"I'll move my hand, but you can't scream." I nodded at Vanessa through the mirror and watched her take her hand away from my face. Her long, sharp, red nails had cut into my skin, I was bleeding. Vanessa stood closely behind me, putting her hands on my shoulders, I looked at her through the mirror, she did the same to me.

"It's you isn't it?" she said, quietly.

"It's really you." I said nothing.

"You need to listen to me now. You go home and you say nothing to anyone. I'll talk to you tomorrow. Are you listening Zoe?" Vanessa dug her hands into my shoulders. I nodded, my body shaking with fear. Vanessa took some tissue from the unit next to us and passed it to me.

"Sort your face out and come downstairs." Vanessa left. I held the tissue to the blood on my face and gently wiped it, tears falling from my eyes. What did I do to deserve this? I had no intention of seeing Vanessa the next day, not with Sandra's funeral coming up. Sandra had to be my focus and priority. I had to deal with one thing at a time.

Chapter 16
Sandra's Time

Blue sky's, green trees, black crows. That's what I remember about that morning. The sky was the bluest I had ever seen, not a single cloud in sight. I was standing outside a small church in Salford, my legs barely able to keep me up. I remember the sun on my face, it was so hot, almost a burning sensation could be felt throughout my entire body. It was a beautiful day, it was the day of Sandra's funeral. I had never known anyone to lose before. I stood feeling lost, alone, like part of me was missing. Jack came with me and tried his best to be there for me but even I didn't know how to be, how to act, what to do, what to say. I was numb.

It was really quiet outside the church. A few birds could be heard and the muffling of other people also attending the funeral. There was a small cemetery attached to the church, to the left and flowers could be seen in every direction. It was really picturesque. I remember saying to Jack,
"Sandra would have loved this." It was peaceful and calm.

More and more people started to arrive and wait outside the church. I didn't know who any of them were. I saw Sandra's son with his girlfriend. I recognised him from his pictures that Sandra had shown me, we acknowledged each other but didn't say anything. I felt so sick, then the worst thing happened, the moment I had been dreading, the hearse arrived.

A green and purple, floral cardboard coffin could be seen through the hearse window. I smiled to myself thinking how much it suited Sandra and how she must have chosen it herself, an environmentally friendly option was definitely her. Purple flowers sat above it with the word '*MUM*' placed on top. When I saw that I burst into tears, it hit me, that's how I felt about her, she was the closest thing I ever had to a mum and she was gone. I was heartbroken. Jack wrapped his arms around me from behind but after a second I shoved him away.

"I'm sorry Jack, I can't do this now." I said, wiping my eyes.

"I'm here." Jack said, letting go of me.

Everyone started making their way inside the church, which was absolutely stunning. I had never been inside a church before, so I really didn't know what to expect. There was a beautiful stained glass window that illuminated with the sun, candles and flowers could be seen at the front with a large canvas picture of Sandra on a stand. The picture must have been from when she was younger. I had never seen it before, but she looked beautiful, such long, curly hair, she really was so naturally beautiful, I was taken back. I didn't know what the service would be like, but I was open to experience everything that Sandra wanted us to. I found out later that Sandra did in fact plan her entire funeral from start to finish. I suppose that's something else that she could have control over. That's something else that she could still do before it was too late. I admired her. I was surprised that she didn't want a wake as such but that was her choice.

Out of nowhere music started to play, a soft instrumental piece, no words but you could almost write your own lyrics to it. Her coffin was then brought in, everyone stood up. I saw her son at the front, he was very composed but you could see the sadness in his eyes. I watched as they walked down the narrow aisle carrying Sandra until they placed her on a black stand at the front of the church. After a few moments, everyone took their seats and the service began. It only lasted about twenty minutes but it was heartfelt and personal. The vicar spoke about Sandra's life, from the moment she was born to the moment she died. I sat comfortably and listened with my whole heart.

VICAR

"Sandra was born and raised in a one bedroom flat in Salford to single parent Amanda Winwick. Amanda was only sixteen when she had Sandra and didn't really have a close family network due to her parents being alcoholics, spending most of their time completely wasted. Sandra was brought up solo by Amanda in bedsits and flats that the government usually helped her get. It was hard but she tried to give Sandra the one thing she could that was completely free-love.

When Sandra eventually went to nursery and then school, Amanda started working as a cleaner to make extra money, starting with neighbours and friends houses, she got known in the area and started building her regular clients before she then settled with an agency. Amanda signed with a rather big cleaning agency and started getting more regular hours and income to support herself and Sandra. Amanda thrived to give her daughter a better life, during school Sandra was also excelling, often bringing home awards and certificates for good behaviour and excellent grades. She expressed interest in teaching and had ambition to study English to eventually become a primary school teacher.

However things took a turn for the worse. Unfortunately when Sandra was just eighteen, having gained an unconditional offer for an English Degree at a London University, Amanda had a stroke, leaving Sandra with no choice but to become her mum's carer. Sandra never questioned whether or not to look after her mum, it was just in her own words *'the right thing to do'*. Sandra didn't get out much during the time she spent looking after her mum with round the clock care, housework and meal prep, there was very little time for anything else. However Sandra's bubbly, infectious personality didn't go unnoticed for very long when local postman Adam started doing the rounds. At just nineteen he took a liking to Sandra, and whilst delivering mail, he managed to make an impression and the two got to know a lot about each other. Now and again Sandra would invite him in for a cuppa, especially in those cold winter months, leading to Adam joining them for dinner and eventually they started a relationship.

A year later they welcomed baby Zack and started a life together in their own little bubble, living in the two bedroom flat that Sandra had grown up in. It was a squeeze but somehow they made it work. Sandra and Adam got married a few years later at the local registry office followed by a buffet at home with a few friends from school and Adam's parents. Although very much in love at the beginning, Sandra and Adam eventually drifted apart and separated after five years together. Not long after Amanda suddenly died of a heart attack leaving just Sandra and Zack together. Sandra followed in her mum's footsteps and started cleaning, leading to a cleaning contract at the industrial estate in Salford. Where she continued to work until present day. Sandra managed to save enough money for a deposit and moved into a three bedroom house, still in Salford, with a front and back garden that she adored pottering around in. It was perfect and a dream for Sandra. Zack loved running around the garden, they had so much space they didn't know what to do with it.

Zack remembers his childhood as happy and content, he was aware his mother often struggled but he never went without. Zack, just like his mum excelled at school and followed in his own business career path, gaining a degree in London where he to this day lives a busy, fulfilled and successful life. Zack says "I am proud of my mum, she taught me how to love, how to work and how to be a good man. I am forever in her debt."

A prayer was then said, everyone joined in and then some music played for reflection, and that was it. All done. Her coffin was picked up and taken away. I adored hearing about Sandra's life, she really was an amazing woman. I was so proud to have known her.
"You alright?" Jack said, putting his arm around me as people were leaving the church. I smiled and stood up to leave. I didn't want to go to the graveside. I sat on a bench and watched from afar. I didn't want to say 'goodbye' and that was the end of it. I felt like I needed to do that on my own, just me and her.

Once the grave side part was over, I asked Jack to take me home. We headed for his car, everything seemed a blur. I was still in shock trying to process everything.
"Zoe, Zoe." I heard from behind me. I turned to find Zack running after me. He handed me a white envelope, sealed with a kiss...literally. It said 'Zoe' in black, capital letters. "I found this with Mum's belongings, she wanted you to have it today." I paused for a moment before taking the envelope from him.
"Thank you." He smiled and left. I held on to it tight and asked Jack for a moment. Jack kissed me on the cheek,

squeezed my hand and told me he would wait in the car for me. I took the envelope and walked to the back of the church, hiding myself away in some overgrown trees and bushes. I sat on a tree stump and stared at the white envelope. I felt sickly, cold, my hands went clammy. I took a deep breath.

"Okay, here we go." I carefully opened the seal and started reading Sandra's words, recognising her writing made me cry straight away, the words became blurry but I focused and made out each word.

Dear Zoe,

STOP the tears! Everything is going to be alright. Okay Missy? Right then, here it goes. I don't think there is any easy way to say this so I'm just going to say it. When you read this letter I won't be around any more. If my son does what I asked, you should get this at my funeral. I know you're probably confused, wondering what the hell is going on? That's alright darling, I'm right here with you and I always will be.

I've had cancer for some time now, long before you contacted me. I didn't want chemo, they said it wouldn't make much difference anyway. But I really didn't want to look in the mirror and see cancer staring back at me in the face everyday so I decided to make the most of my time here and when it ends, it ends. I have felt myself getting weaker these last few months, the last time I went to the doctors, he told me I didn't have long left. I am so sorry I didn't tell you Hun. But this is how I wanted it. I wanted it to be my choice, my way. I hope you understand Zoe. It was my way of dealing with it.

I guess then I need to tell you how I feel about you. My girl. You make me so proud. From the moment I saw you on the doorstep, I never stopped thinking about you, wondering about you, to be a part of your adult life means so much to me. You have no idea how much I hoped to be there for you when you find out the truth. Which my girl, you have to do! Do it for me and do it for you. You go and finish what we started. I promise I'm right behind you.

Tell Jack, he better look after you!

I love you Zoe. I love you.

I held the letter close to my chest and quietly sobbed. Closing my eyes, imagining her sitting beside me. I opened my eyes that were full of water, blinking to try and clear my vision. I knew what I had to do. I held the letter tight in my hands and made my way to Sandra's grave. There wasn't anyone around any more. I could see Jack's car in the distance, parked up on the side street. It was very quiet. I walked to where Sandra had just been buried, it was covered in fresh soil, placed on top were some of the flowers from her coffin. I couldn't believe she was in there, it was so surreal. I looked down at the soil and smiled, wiping tears from my cheeks.

"I had a whole in my heart my whole life and somehow having you with me, it slowly started to heal. I'll find out the truth, the whole truth. I promise. But to me, you'll always be the only Mum I ever needed. I love you."
and then I left.

Chapter 17
The Flashback

After Sandra's funeral I had put off seeing Vanessa for as long as I could. I was so close to the truth that I started to wonder if it was even worth it. I could just leave? Start again? Be successful? That could be my freedom? But I remembered Sandra's letter to me. I couldn't give up, if not for me, I needed to do it for her, she wanted to know the truth as much as me. I took a week off work to really get myself together. I realised I was never going to be ready for the truth but I had come this far. Giving up wasn't an option.

The day had finally come to see Vanessa, after what I had discovered at Megan's house. We had arranged to meet at work. Vanessa had closed the salon for a few days due to some maintenance that needed to be done, she messaged me when the workmen had gone, she wanted me to go round when there was no one else there, for obvious reasons. When I arrived at work my heart was pounding. I was stepping directly into the unknown and there was no one left in the world that knew what was going on, not even Jack. Vanessa was standing with a clipboard scribbling something down. There were tools everywhere, new styling units were partly fitted, dust sheets all over the floor, it was unrecognisable. Vanessa looked well, she always did, wearing a black trouser suit, hair tied back in a wavy ponytail and of course really high heels. Her outfit shouted *'boss lady'*.

As much as Vanessa did scare me and I didn't want to like her, I couldn't help but admire her. I mean everyone wanted to be like Vanessa, right?
We stepped into her office where she locked the door behind me.
"Don't worry, it's just so we don't get disturbed." she said, getting me to sit down on the sofa. I watched Vanessa go over to the water dispenser, she filled two small cups and brought one over to me.
"Thanks." I was nervous. I took a sip and placed it on the glass table in front of us trying to stop my hand from shaking. Vanessa did the same. It was silent for what seemed like a very long time before Vanessa finally started to speak to me.
"That bloody photo." she said, almost nervously laughing. But I didn't find it amusing, not one bit.
"I guess this day was inevitable." she continued.
"I just want the truth Vanessa."

I don't know what I was expecting Vanessa to tell me, but nothing could prepare me for what she was about to say, nothing at all.

VANESSA

"I first saw Megan at school. I went to pick Daniel up one evening from football practice, they came around the corner together. Daniel had his arm around her, she was so beautiful, effortless even, such long, wavy hair. They kissed each other, they must have only been around twelve, thirteen, something like that, so innocent, so young. But I saw the way my Daniel looked at her. I knew from that moment that he was besotted by her. He was smitten like all boys are but I knew how he felt, even at that age.

They started dating when they went to secondary school, they made it all official, told everyone, friends, family, they updated their social media, everyone knew. Megan stayed with us a lot because she didn't get on with her own parents, she stayed in a separate room- obviously. I really wasn't comfortable with them sharing, not that young. Daniel used to ask me to help him cook for her, he was a romantic little thing, always wanted her to feel special. Richard didn't know if it would last, but I did.

After a few years of them dating, Richard really hoped it was the *real deal* too. We were very fond of Megan, and Daniel was becoming the most perfect gentleman. On Megan's fourteenth birthday, we had a BBQ for her in our garden. It wasn't a massive gathering, just family, mainly ours and friends but it was really special. I don't think anyone had ever made a fuss of her before, she was so grateful.

It was a really warm day, everyone was in the party spirit, enjoying the sun, but towards the end of it Megan had said she wasn't feeling well. So I took her to the spare room for a lay down. A few hours passed and I could hear her throwing up in the bathroom. I checked on her, looked after her and insisted she stopped the night so I could keep my eye on her. I asked if she had been unwell before and she said that she had experienced sickness on and off for the last month. I tucked her into bed and told her that if she still felt sick the next day, I would phone school and take her to the doctors. Megan didn't sleep much and was up most of the night. I did what I could but of course Daniel wanted to look after her.

The next day I managed to get an appointment at the doctors and I drove her there myself. When we got there she looked worse, very pale and fragile. The doctors did some tests and told us they would be in touch. Everything went on as normal. Megan and Daniel were still very happy, doing well at school, all of us spending time together. About four days later the doctors got in touch with me and wanted to speak to Megan in person. So once again I drove her to the doctors. We sat with Dr Amy Smith, I won't ever forget what she went on to say... "Megan love, your blood tests have come back and show that you're pregnant..."
My heart stopped, staring at this doctor. Megan was in complete shock, denial. "No, No, No." she screamed. I took hold of her hand and tried to be there for her. I just

couldn't get my head around it. I mean she was only fourteen years old, she was just a baby herself. But I thought- no this is family now, whatever it takes. The rest of the conversation with the doctor was a bit of a blur. I was almost blaise until we got into the car to go home. "Right, let's get back and work out how we are going to tell Daniel and Richard." I said to her, my hands gripping the steering wheel. I was trying to keep calm myself, trying to focus my mind so I could be there for her, for them. Megan started howling, smacking her head against the window, I had to restrain her to calm her down. "Stop it! Stop it. You're not alone!" I tried telling her, she was just a mess.

"The baby, it's not Daniels." she screamed.

In that moment my world stood still. I felt completely numb. How could it not be Daniels? Who was this little tramp sitting in my car? I was furious! That's what I remember thinking, like I didn't know this girl at all. I grabbed Megan's seatbelt and tied it around her, clicking it in place so tight that she couldn't move. I drove off as quickly as I could possibly go without getting stopped. I didn't have a plan, I didn't know what I was going to do. I couldn't think straight. Megan was sobbing, telling me I was hurting her.

"Do me a favour Megan. Shut the fuck up." I said, absolutely disgusted with her. I drove to a neglected area of Manchester, the houses were derelict, lots of graffiti on the walls, mess and rubble everywhere. I stared straight ahead, I could hear Megan trying to quietly sob in pain but I couldn't bring myself to look at her. I kept thinking about Daniel, my beautiful baby boy, he was going to be heartbroken.

"Vanessa please undo the seatbelt." Megan pleaded with me, but I didn't listen. I didn't really care.

"Tell me the truth now." I was so angry with her. Megan was in pain, I could see that she couldn't speak properly, struggling to get her words out.

"I'm sorry. I love Daniel."

"Don't you dare say his name! Who's is it?"

"This boy at school, it just happened. I didn't mean to, we were drinking at his."

"So you have been to his house?" You have been drinking?! Who even are you?"

"Vanessa please."

"How many times? How many times did you cheat on my boy?!"

"Just once I promise, I didn't know what I was doing. I never thought this would happen. "Please Vanessa. I am so sorry."

I unclipped the seatbelt. Megan let out the biggest gasp and it took her a while to get herself together.

"So you slept with some random person because you had a few cheap ciders and didn't know how to handle yourself."

"What are you going to do?" I didn't answer her. I drove us home in complete and utter silence.

172

"Get out." I let us in the house and told her to sit down. Obviously Daniel was at school. I poured myself a glass of red and sat on the sofa in the living room, right across from Megan who looked a right state. We both kept watching the clock, waiting for the door to go. Eventually it did, Daniel walked through the door in his uniform, rucksack over his shoulder, not a care in the world. Daniel could tell that something wasn't right. He was very confused.

"What's wrong?" his little voice said.

"Sit down, love. Megan's got something to tell you."

"Mum."

"Just sit down." Daniel reluctantly sat on the sofa next to me. It was a large L-shape at the time, and we all sat away from each other. You could have cut the tension with a knife. There was a lot of silence and stares from all of us until Megan got the courage to tell Daniel what she had done.

"I'm pregnant." she mumbled. I won't ever forget the look on Daniel's face, he didn't know whether to laugh or cry. He looked over at me, I could see his lip go and his eyes started to fill with water. He looked over to Megan. "But we haven't even..." Megan burst out crying, Daniel realising what that meant, grabbed his bag and left the house. He didn't come back for hours. Megan wanted to leave to go after him but I wasn't letting her leave my sight. Megan didn't move until about five hours later when Daniel came back home. His eyes were bloodshot red with crying. His white school shirt was filthy and his hands were bloody. He had been in his tree house, obviously punching the walls. He was so small and looked so sad and helpless. He stood shaking in the middle of the living room.

"I'll stand by you." he said to Megan. Megan was shocked and so was I. He looked over to me. "Mum, that's it please." I nodded. He was my boy, of course I nodded. I left them to it, I'm not sure what was said between them two.

Later that night once Megan had gone, Daniel came to find me. I was doing my hair after the longest, much needed bubble bath. I remember him sitting on the end of my bed and taking the deepest breath.

"Help me." he said. "Help me get rid of this baby. I can't do it." he sobbed all night in my arms, just sobbed his little heart out. He kept telling me how much he loved Megan and couldn't lose her but he couldn't bring up a baby that wasn't his. I mean, could you blame him? I didn't know what to do, not really. But I did know I had to help him, he was my baby. I couldn't see him hurt, so we worked on Megan. We convinced her the best thing to do was to give the baby up, telling her she was too young to have a baby, that it would be life changing. I wasn't lying, neither of them were ready for it, and with the decision already made to not tell the baby's dad, she agreed- eventually.

Megan spent most of her pregnancy in isolation at our house, she didn't cope with being pregnant well. I was working at my mum's salon back then, just helping out before I would eventually take over, and so I looked after her, even took her out of school. Richard didn't want anything to do with it, he distanced himself from all of us over that period, working all the hours he could, going out with his mates when he was at home. It wasn't an easy thing to do but at the time it felt like the right thing to do, for all of us.

Eight months went past, and one night I heard screaming coming from Megan's room, her waters had broken. That's when it felt real, she was terrified, we all were. Daniel never came into the room, Richard was away working, it was just Megan and I. Megan was only in labour for eight hours, she gave birth to a beautiful baby girl at 3.45am on Friday 18th February 2004, weighing just over 7 pounds.

Megan never held you Zoe, she was very poorly after the birth. Once I saw you, I panicked. You were so tiny, so innocent, you didn't ask for any of this. I honestly think I went into shock. I cleaned you up and wrapped you in a big fluffy blanket that I just grabbed off the bed. I carried you downstairs and put you in a small brown box that a delivery had come in a few days before. It was actually a delivery from the salon, Mum named it after me before she even had me you know. Anyway I was on autopilot, not really present. It was like an outer body experience. I was shaking, I remember grabbing my car keys from my handbag and I couldn't keep them still. I noticed some pictures on the side unit near the front door.

Daniel had developed them, four small passport size photos of Megan he had taken. I took one and wrote on the back of it, my hand smudging the writing. I hid it with you in the box and I carried you to the car. I drove around with you crying, I didn't know what to do, it was horrible. Then I saw a sign for a Social Service Unit, I followed it until I came to it and...

Vanessa went silent, putting her hand to her mouth.

"Oh my god. I remember. I put you on the doorstep near the entrance, I knew someone would find you. But there was a woman, when I was rushing back to the car, she asked after me. It was her wasn't it? It was Sandra?"

Silence.

Chapter 18
The Truth, The Whole Truth, And Nothing But The Truth

       I sat in complete and utter shock with what Vanessa had just told me. One family scandal defined my entire start in life. I wasn't even given a chance to try and be loved. I was literally just disregarded like the inconvenience I was. No one wanted me. Did I blame Megan? I didn't know. She was young, stupid, I wasn't planned, I know that, but she didn't even hold me...

"Zoe." Vanessa shook me.

"I am so sorry." I didn't even know what to say. I had no words.

"Zoe." Vanessa raised her voice a little.

"What Vanessa? What do you want me to say? You want me to thank you for telling me the truth. You left me on a doorstep, I was a baby! A baby that you just delivered, how could you do that and just get on with your perfect little life?! Do you have any idea of the life I have had? And now to be told that I wasn't wanted by anyone, I was just dumped like a bag of rubbish, are you kidding me!!" I got up and left as quickly as I could, Vanessa tried to pull me back, grabbing my arm.

"Let me go Vanessa." I pushed her off me and ran out of the salon. I needed air, I needed time to think. I needed to figure out what the hell to do.

Back in my bedsit, after avoiding multiple calls from Vanessa, I stood naked looking into the bathroom mirror. I was reminded of all those months before when I stood in the very same place, longing for the truth. The truth was not what I wanted to hear. It wasn't even a bittersweet moment, it was just bitter. I remember the girl that stood before the mirror at the beginning of my story, looking through a dirty, grubby reflection. My surroundings felt like they had been forgotten, old and dated. I was pretty much the same but at least it was all real. At least I was true to myself. Fast forward to that moment and everything seemed so fake and false. Even Jack had no real idea of who I was. The truth was all I ever wanted and yet it was suffocating me. I looked around at my boudoir surroundings and laughed to myself, not believing my luck. If only the truth wasn't so hard to swallow, I would have done pretty well for myself.

I turned off the hot tap that was going at speed in the background. The hot water started to steam into the room and I could no longer see my reflection in the mirror. I sat on the toilet seat and hovered my finger over the perfectly still water that filled the bath high. It was too hot even to touch, but I slowly started making ripple effects with my finger. It burnt, it hurt but in a way it was nice, it was a release, at least it felt like that at the time. After a few moments it didn't hurt any more, my fingers just felt numb. I eventually submerged myself into the hot water, allowing water to spill over the side. I closed my eyes and let the water fully cover me as I laid at the bottom of the bath. I could feel all my hair covering my face. I could have drifted off in that moment, honestly I could. It was so quiet and peaceful. I just wanted peace. All of a sudden I heard a large bang. I jumped up immediately, water everywhere.

"Hello." I shouted, whilst getting out of the bath and wrapping a towel around me. I was startled and worried. I walked into the main part of my bedsit, water dripping off me and going all over the floor. There was no one there, the door was locked, the windows were locked. It was just bizarre. The sound was so loud, it definitely came from my bedsit. I tightened the towel around me and headed back to the bathroom when something shiny caught my eye. I had a white shelving unit under my window with a glass vase sat on top and some fresh flowers neatly placed inside. On the bottom shelf was my silver tin with the picture of Megan in it that was left with me as a baby. It was open on the floor, the picture a few feet away. There was no way it could have fallen and even if it did, the sound it would have made would have been nothing like the loud bang I heard before. It might sound ridiculous but

I instantly felt like it was Sandra, reminding me not to give up. It was her way of telling me that I wasn't alone. I was grieving so maybe it was all nonsense, but believing it was Sandra gave me the comfort and strength that I desperately needed.

A few days later I decided to go back to work. I didn't really have a choice. I needed the money to pay my rent and bills, I was no longer getting help from the government since accepting Vanessa's offer of a promotion. When I arrived all the staff were confused. I saw them looking me up and down like I needed a reality check, rolling their eyes at each other as if to say *who does she think she is*' if only they knew. I hung up my coat and sat down at the reception desk where I got on with my job. I went above and beyond for the clients and staff, after all they didn't deserve a shit time all because I was having a shit life. Vanessa wasn't working that day but one of the staff members had clearly messaged her to let her know I was at work, because she came rushing through the door fifteen minutes before my shift finished.
"Zoe please can I talk to you?" she said, hovering over the counter, trying to be discreet. Vanessa knew that all the staff were watching, I imagined she found the whole thing embarrassing.
"I just want to work." I said, typing away on the computer.
"Zoe, please we can't go on like this."
"Fine."

Vanessa ran her fingers through her hair and headed towards her office.

"Can you bring me an ice cold sparkling water." I heard her say to Amy.

The time flashed by and soon it was gone 5pm. I finished what I was doing, filled out the handover sheet and went to Vanessa's office. Here we go again I thought to myself. I knocked and walked straight in, I think we had gone past the point of all formalities. Vanessa stood, staring out the window in a bit of a daze.

"Vanessa."

"Zoe Sit down."

"No, I'm alright."

"I just..."

"Just what?"

"I want to know what are you going to do? Now you know the truth." I just stared at her, she was unbelievable, she didn't care about me at all, just herself and her reputation.

"I guess I will need to talk to Megan."

"NO!" Vanessa shouted. "You can't."

"I can do whatever I want Vanessa. You can't keep controlling and messing with my life."

"Zoe, she's not ready for this, she's delicate."

"She's delicate! I am eighteen years old and have to deal with all this shit alone!" I was so mad with her saying that to me.

"I know, I'm sorry but she could have a breakdown! Chloe needs her mum."

"Oh wow. You really are a cow aren't you? I guess I never did need a mum, did I? You made sure of that!"

"Zoe! Please at least let me tell her. Please."

"Fine have it your way but I want this over with. I need to move on with my life." I left abruptly.

I went to The Plant Pot not even necessarily to see Jack, I just needed a drink. Jack and I were alright but I didn't really know what we were. It felt at that time that it was a real effort to keep on top of anything with him because I had so much personal shit going on.

"Pint please." I said to Jack when I arrived. I sat at the bar and held my head, I had the worst tension headache of all times. Jack was working on his own, the other guy helping him out was on his second dinner break, he was outside having a cig when I arrived. There weren't many people in, maybe a few students? I wasn't really paying attention. I didn't even notice Jack was being different with me until later in the evening when I asked for another drink.

"Is this what it's going to be like all night?" he said, frustrated.

"What?"

"You haven't spoken to me at all apart from to ask me for a drink."

"Jack seriously, what's up?"

"Don't worry about it."

"No, come on."

"Fine. Where have you been? I mean since you went to Megan's I am lucky if I even get a reply."

"Jack I'm sorry, I'm just..."

"Yes, you're going through stuff. You know I cared about Sandra too. I am trying my best for you and all you do is push me away."

"I can't do this."

"You're walking away?"

"Yes Jack, yes I am, before I say something I'll regret."

"What does that even mean?"

I walked off and left him without an answer. Where the hell did that come from? I was literally back to square one, completely alone in the world, that's certainly how it felt. I really cared about Jack and didn't want to lose him as well. But I just couldn't see it working out, maybe I really did have to close the book on him. I really wasn't sure.

Chapter 19
The Last Supper

A month had passed and nothing had happened. Vanessa kept telling me that it wasn't the right time, that I just had to be patient. I was losing patience and fast. By that point I was completely ignoring Megan's messages too. We were never really friends, I know it's harsh to say, but we never hung out in coffee shops or posh bars. It was a friendship we had built purely through a connection we found at work. Obviously I knew now that it wasn't just a random connection, she was my mum. Megan did appear to genuinely care about me though, she always wanted to check in to make sure everything was alright. That's why I couldn't bring myself to reply to her, because I just didn't know what to say. I didn't want to engage in a conversation with her and say something I shouldn't. Especially with Vanessa telling me how emotionally fragile she was, but it was getting so ridiculous.

Jack and I had also completely drifted apart, a few casual messages were exchanged but it never led anywhere. I hoped at that time that it wouldn't be the end of Jack and I, but I couldn't make him a priority. I had too much I needed to sort out. One day I planned to go to Jack, give him the biggest hug and tell him the truth. Unfortunately I never got that chance.

"Vanessa!" I barged into her office one evening after I finished my shift. I gave up caring.

"You can't just." Vanessa rushed up from behind her desk.

"What? When are you going to tell Megan? This is stupid now, it's been months."

"I'm waiting for the right time."

"There isn't a right time, there never will be."

"I know you're frustrated."

"Understatement."

"But I am trying my best here."

"I don't think you are! I think..." the door to Vanessa's office suddenly swung open. It was Megan, we both froze on the spot.

"Everything alright?" Megan asked, trying to settle Chloe in the pram.

"You asked me to drop your tablet off." Megan said, reaching into her bag clearly confused.

"Yes, thanks." Vanessa took it off Megan and walked to the back of the office with it."

"Zoe how are you?" she said, again looking genuinely concerned.

"Yeah fine."

"Have you changed phones? I've messaged you a few times but..."

"Oh sorry yeah I did."

"I'll have to get your new number." I smiled just staring at her. Megan did actually look like me. I had never noticed it before but she had my freckles under her eyes. Her hair was the same as mine too, well my natural hair, she was beautiful. I felt in some ways I was doing what Megan had to do when she first started dating Daniel. Megan found herself in this high class world full of opportunity, she had to learn to adapt to it. Maybe that's why she always got on with me, because she could be herself? She could be real and drop the pretence.

"So…" Megan tried to ask.

"So what?" Vanessa said.

"What were you two talking about?" Vanessa and I looked at each other. Vanessa was about to speak but I cut her off.

"Actually I was just saying how much I enjoyed your dinner party."

"Awe thank you, it was such a good night wasn't it?"

"Yeah I didn't want it to end."

"Let's do it again then!" Megan started getting giddy, her eyes lighting up like a child.

"I don't think…" Vanessa tried to stop it from happening but she could just do one.

"You free Friday, around 7pm?" Megan asked.

"Sure am."

"Fantastic! Can't wait."

"Me too."

"Right, let me get this little one home. I'll tell Daniel when he finishes work. See you both soon."

"Bye." I said, Vanessa smiled but she was furious.

"What the hell do you think you are doing?! This is my family."

"Actually Megan is my family and Chloe is technically my half sister. You have until Friday or I am telling her everything."

"I won't let you destroy us."

"You have no choice Vanessa." I left feeling a little smug, but I was scared to death. If Vanessa didn't do what she had been promising me, then it was all down to me. Friday was going to be a night to remember.

It was a beautiful table, she outdid herself, it was flawless. Bright blue and silver was the colour scheme on that particular night. It was elegant- of course it was. A sparkly silver candle stood neatly, lit in the centre of the table. Pure white napkins in blue napkin rings sat in the centre of all the white plates that were sat in front of us. Blue and silver table confetti sprinkled like snow all over the table and the most beautiful crystal studded champagne holder with four flute glasses sat to the left hand side of the table. What a shame it was all about to be ruined.

I was sat in-between Megan and Richard, leaving Daniel and Vanessa in my full view. If looks could kill, I would have died right there in that moment. Vanessa was doing everything she could to intimidate me but I was determined not to let her get to me. I had to be strong. The conversation was flowing, again mainly thanks to Richard who was keeping it all light hearted and fun. The men were well away, laughing and joking. I laughed when everyone else laughed and did my best to *'play along'*- for now.

"Right, let's get this open." Daniel said, reaching across the table for the champagne. Megan handed us all a flute, Daniel prepared the champagne, everyone cheered. He filled our glasses like the expert he seemed, it was always poured so perfectly, he held his glass up.

"A toast... to another great evening."

"Another great evening." Everyone touched glasses and took a sip. I could feel Vanessa looking at me over her glass, I looked at her. It was more than tense. Megan and I managed to share a few laughs under Vanessa's watchful eye.

"You alright love, you're very quiet." I heard Richard say quietly to Vanessa, she never answered him.

"Right, I'll go check on dinner. "Megan got up and left the table shortly followed by Daniel who decided to help whilst getting another bottle of champagne.

"Toilet time." Richard joked moments later, all ready he was a little tipsy. Vanessa and I were alone.

"Don't you dare say anything! Vanessa whispered across the table to me. There wasn't much time for me to respond or Vanessa to say anything else because Daniel soon followed with a large, oval, steaming hot plate.

"This smells amazing," he said. He placed it on the table followed by another dish that Megan followed with. When they both took the lids off, the most beautiful seafood platter could be seen with all the trimmings. There were lobsters, prawns, mussels, oysters, crabs, scallops, you name it, it was there. Megan brought fresh salad and vegetables out too, it looked divine. I had never eaten seafood before so I didn't really know if I liked it. I wasn't used to seeing food in front of me with eyes staring back at me. I always used to think seafood platters were for posh, stuck up people. I had only ever seen seafood platters on TV and in magazines. But I was excited to try something new. Richard came rushing in rubbing his hands together.

"Tuck in everyone." Megan said, happy and content. I saw Daniel put his arm around her and kiss her cheek. They were happy, they were so happy. Everyone took their seats to enjoy the meal, large serving spoons were dotted around the table so everyone could help themselves. I remember the first thing I tried was the crab with some garlic and butter sauce, it was incredible. I could almost taste and smell the ocean sea, spray and air, it was that fresh. I ended up trying a little bit of everything and I was not disappointed, it was such an amazing food experience for me.

Vanessa was struggling, she couldn't bring herself to eat much. I saw her just keep filling up her champagne flute to sit and stare at me. I tucked into my food more, appreciating the moment, not knowing what would unfold.

I waited until everyone had enjoyed the food, the last thing I wanted was for everything to go to waste.

Once everyone had put down their knives and forks, I felt like the time had come. I took one last look around the table. Megan happy, smiling across at Daniel, Richard laughing to his own joke and Vanessa, who sat like she had just been shat on. I took a deep breath knowing that once I started, there was no going back.

"I just wanted to thank you all." I said.

"Awe what for?" Megan touched my hand with hers.

"Letting me in and allowing me to feel like part of your family."

"That's so nice Zoe." Daniel said, whilst tucking back into his lobster bisque.

"Have you ever had anyone from the salon over before for dinner?" I asked.

"Actually, no. You must be the chosen one." Richard said, howling.

"The chosen one?" I was trying to lead the conversation to a point when I felt like I could say what I had to say.

"This is divine." Vanessa rushed to say, aiming so hard to sway the conversation.

"You have such a beautiful house and Chloe, she really is a credit to you." I didn't stop.

"Thank you darling. We are very lucky. Chloe can be a handful, but we wouldn't change her for the world." Megan said, not taking her eyes off the baby monitor that sat at the side of us with a warm smile.

"Did you always want a baby?"

"More champagne anyone?" Vanessa stood up, knocking her knife on the floor as she reached across the table to take the champagne. No one answered, all engrossed in the conversation.

"Yes I did. Daniel, not at first but when Chloe came along, it just felt right. What about you? You and Jack thought about it?"

"Me? No. I don't think motherhood is for me." I laughed.

"Jack alright about that?" Daniel asked, trying to genuinely engage in the conversation.

"Actually Jack and I are taking a break for now."

"Sorry to hear that." Daniel seemed sincere.

"I've just got a lot going on in my life that I need to prioritise."

"Sandra... I understand." Megan said, giving my hand a squeeze, she was always so supportive of me, always trying to be there for me, I don't even think she realised she was doing it. I tuck hold of Megan's hand.

"Yeah Sandra... and you."

"Me?" Megan was still smiling, oblivious.

"I think we should clear some of these plates." Vanessa was getting more and more flustered.

"It's always been about you, Megan." At that point Daniel and Richard had stopped eating completely and just stared at me too, having heard the tail end of the conversation.

"Okay I'm confused love."

"Zoe stop this." Vanessa said, raising her voice at me.

"What's going on?" Megan asked me, her smile fading away. I let go of her hand and looked at Vanessa before looking back at Megan. I could feel my eyes start to water. I took a deep breath.

"None of this. None of this is real."

"I think someone's had too much to drink." Richard said, putting more food on his plate.

"Zoe are you alright?" Megan put her arm on my shoulder.

"Actually yeah, I think I am. I have been waiting for this moment my whole life."

"Zoe a word." Vanessa stood behind me with her hands on my shoulders, I could feel her sharp nails digging into me.

"Will someone just please tell me what's going on?" Megan was starting to get anxious.

"I came into your life on purpose. I planned it all with Sandra, she helped me."

"Helped you do what?"

"Become a different person. I bleach my hair, I straighten it, I fake tan, I wear makeup, I buy expensive clothes. I got a job at Vanessa's salon, it was all an act, all part of the plan."

"I don't understand."

"None of us bloody do." Daniel said, sitting back in his chair stuffed with the food and confused as well.

"I needed to find out the truth about me, about my family."

"Zoe, you're not making any sense," Megan said.

Vanessa's grip got tighter and tighter on my shoulders. My eyes started to weep with the pain, but I had to say it, I had too.

"Megan, you're my mum." I screamed.

Chapter 20
The Aftermath

The table was silent. Megan went white, Daniel and Richard were looking at each other in shock and Vanessa had let go of me and had gone over to stand behind Daniel. I sat longing for Megan to wrap her arms around me. A few minutes went past and no one said anything.
"I promise it's true." my voice was small and shaky.
"Megan." I said.
"Just shut up." she had never spoken to me like that before, she held her hand up to me suggesting she wanted me to give her space. More minutes went by in silence. I couldn't look at anyone anymore, I just looked down to the floor but I could feel everyone staring at me. Eventually Megan turned to me in her chair. I looked at her, deep in the eyes.
"You think I'm your mum? My baby's dead." she was so cold, like her entire body had been taken over. Her face went blank, like she wasn't even looking at me, she was looking straight through me.
"Dead? What?" I looked over at Vanessa who had her head in her hands, I didn't understand.
"Zoe, I would like you to leave." Daniel said, rushing up to support Megan. Megan pushed Daniel away and grabbed my hands.

"How did you know about the baby before?" Megan had changed again, she was in complete and utter shock, her mood kept changing within seconds.

"That baby was me." I cried. "I didn't want it to happen like this but Vanessa..."

"You're part of this." Daniel shouted to his mum.

"What the hell is going on Mum?" Daniel was getting angrier.

"Vanessa!" Richard said, for the first time with some authority to his voice.

"Vanessa, please tell them who I am. Tell them the truth." I literally begged her. Vanessa just stood there, before taking a seat back at the table.

"I am so sorry... she's crazy." Vanessa said, composed, in control.

"What?" I stood up, slamming my hands on the table, some of the champagne flutes fell over, soaking what was left of the food.

"I tried to talk her out of this ludicrous idea but..."

"My baby is dead." Megan had lost it, she just kept repeating those words.

"Megan, it's me. I am your baby." I yelled, pointing at myself hard in the chest.

"Enough." Daniel got my arms from behind and dragged me out of the house.

"No! Megan I need to talk to you." I yelled.

Daniel chucked me outside, swearing at me. I fell on the step and knocked my shoe off, picking it up I pleaded with him to listen.

"You never come near us again." he shut the door in my face.

"I'm telling the truth." I said, sobbing to myself.

Why did no one believe me? Why did Megan say her baby was dead? Why did Vanessa lie? What was happening? I didn't understand why I was the one crying, cold on the pavement, thrown to the floor with nothing but hate and anger directed towards me. All I tried to do was tell the truth. Something wasn't right, something felt very, very wrong. Vanessa lied to me, there was more to this than meets the eye.

I could hear shouting from inside the house as I leant on the water fountain to put my shoe back on. I felt useless, worthless, pointless, herded out of the house like an animal. Was I defeated? Absolutely not. I had nothing left in the world to lose. I walked to the back of the house and sat on a bench that had almost disappeared into large bushes and floral flowers. I could just about see into the kitchen. The house was lit up and parts of the garden but I was confident I couldn't be seen. I took my phone out of my bag and went into 'contacts' scrolling through until I found Jack. I hovered my finger over his name for a few minutes. Do I call him? Do I not? I hadn't spoken to Jack properly in ages. But I needed him, I needed him so much.

NO! I said to myself. I couldn't do it, I couldn't get close to him that night to ditch him again on another. It wasn't fair, he deserved better. I switched my phone off and put it in my bag, out of sight, out of mind. The house was still brightly lit. I didn't know what I was doing, I just knew I couldn't leave, it wasn't an option. I checked my watch and it read 9.45pm, it was getting darker and colder.

My eyes wandered around the garden, looking at all the silver lights lit perfectly in their chosen place, flowers watered and grown to perfection, their colours could just about be made out under the lights. The bushes and trees gently blowing in the light breeze, the lawn neater than neat. It was perfect, utter perfection. There was a large white shed at the back of the garden. I thought about walking over to it. It might have been open? At least it would have been warmer?

All of a sudden I heard the patio doors swing open. It was Megan followed quickly by Daniel. I rushed up and hid behind the bench. Megan stood lighting a cigarette, I didn't even know she smoked. Daniel stood behind her, his head in his hands. He looked desperate to hold her but Megan seemed tense, uptight. I remained still and silent. I could not get caught.
"Don't you touch me." I heard Megan yell at Daniel. I slowly turned to face them more, peaking through the back of the bench.
"Why are you taking this out on me? Zoe was your friend!"

"Don't you dare, don't you dare."

"I have no idea where any of that came from either."

"Something isn't right about this. Your mum knew something."

"Oh so now it's my mum's fault?!

"She was acting strange all night."

"Was she? She told you! Zoe is crazy, obsessed."

"Yeah well Zoe knew things, things she shouldn't know."

"She's just a messed up kid that's become attached to you. You let her into your life, our life, our home. She's besotted by you."

"I cannot go through this again."

"Hey come here, I'm here, like I always have been. Please don't shut me out." Daniel wrapped Megan in his arms. I watched Megan uncomfortably move away from Daniel, she threw her cig that had already gone out to the floor. She started walking away back into the house before she turned back to him.

"Maybe ask yourself why I let an eighteen year old kid into OUR life Daniel. Don't come to bed tonight."

"Megan!!" Megan slammed the door behind her. I was shocked it didn't wake Chloe up, it made me jump and I was watching. Daniel picked up the cigarette from the floor and lit it, he took a long drag looking up at the sky as he did. Not long after his phone started ringing in his pocket, he looked at it and looked over his shoulder back into the house. He shouted 'Megan' a few times which I thought was odd before he answered it.

"What the hell just happened?" Daniel said down the phone, clearly fuming but trying to keep his voice quiet. "So it's true then? How did she find us? I can't speak about this here, it's too risky. Come tomorrow morning at 8am. Megan's taking Chloe to a play date if it still happens. You should have warned me Mum. What the hell have you done!!" Daniel hung up the phone.

That was it, he threw his cigarette to the floor stomping on it with rage before heading inside himself and again slamming the door shut. My head was mashed, I couldn't believe what I was hearing. So there were more lies?! But it wasn't just Vanessa, it was Vanessa and Daniel. I was beginning to believe that Megan really did think her daughter was dead after all. What happened all them years ago? What did Vanessa and Daniel do?!

I quietly and slowly walked to the shed at the back of the garden, it had a huge brown padlock on it, it was locked. I looked back to the house and saw the light in the main bedroom go on, the light's downstairs were still all on too. There wasn't time to hesitate or think, I rushed over to the patio doors leading into the kitchen. I put my hand on the door handle and pushed it, it opened. I had a moment where I couldn't believe my luck 'it wasn't locked'. I quietly closed the door behind me and stood in the kitchen, adrenaline rushing all around my body. I couldn't believe I was actually standing in the house. I was worried if I was to get caught I would end up getting arrested, but I needed to hear that conversation between Daniel and Vanessa. It was the only way I was ever going to get to the real truth. I took off my shoes and walked into the living room space, I could hear Megan and Daniel upstairs. Megan was telling Daniel she didn't want to sleep with him, I kept hearing her say,

"Go sleep in the spare room or I will." They argued for some time until Chloe started crying.

"Well done Daniel." I heard Megan scream at him before a door slammed shut, so I assumed she went into Chloe's room. I saw Daniel in the hallway from downstairs as I tried to make my way around the bottom part of the house.

"Shit." I really needed to find somewhere to hide. I went back into the living room and scouted the room, everything was so neatly placed, there was nowhere to hide without being seen. I could hear Daniel making his way down the stairs, I was panicking, running through the house back to the kitchen. I almost slipped on the floor, I stood at the patio doors to go back outside but I knew I would never get that opportunity again. I turned behind me looking at the kitchen unit, the island space and the sofa area with all Chloe's toys. The toys were placed in boxes, neatly put away, stacked on top of each other like always but this time there was a white, fluffy blanket, hanging over the sofa. It would be a squeeze, I thought but I had to try. I rushed to the sofa, laid on my side and rolled under it, squeezing my body through the small gap under the sofa. I just about had enough time to pull the blanket over the sofa so the gap couldn't be seen before Daniel walked in. I could feel my heart pounding as I listened to him pottering around the kitchen.

The floor was so cold, I could feel my body shivering. I heard Daniel open the fridge and grab himself a beer before leaving out the patio doors. He kept coming back and forth all night. I kept nodding off then waking up with every slight sound or movement. My eyes were so heavy, so tired. It was getting darker and darker and darker, before long I was in complete darkness.

"Daniel. Daniel." I jumped up and banged my head, it took me a few moments to remember where I was and what I was doing. I carefully lifted the blanket to one side so I could see what was going on. I saw Daniel sat on a breakfast stool, clasped over the island unit, clearly he had got drunk and passed out.
"Well at least you made yourself useful." Megan said, holding Chloe, still angry from the previous night.
"What?" Daniel was slowly starting to come round.
"Don't be like that Meg."
"This is you all over isn't it. Anytime there's a problem, get drunk, pass-out, hope it will all go away."
"That's not fair."
"Yeah well, life is not fair." Megan put Chloe in her high chair and reached into the fridge for a yoghurt to give her. Daniel tried to interact with Chloe but she resisted.

"How long are you going to keep blaming me for?" Daniel was irritated and started to raise his voice a little.

"I didn't ask for this either."

"I don't know Daniel, something doesn't feel right any more."

"With me? Seriously Megan, we've been together forever, you really think I could keep anything from you?"

"I don't know Daniel." Megan cleaned Chloe up and carried her out of the high chair.

"See you later." And with that Megan had gone. Moments later I heard the front door bang shut, Daniel hit the kitchen counter with his fist.

"Fuck!" he yelled.

He took his phone and held it up to his ear after tapping away on it briefly,

"Yes, she's gone." he slammed the phone down next to him and disappeared for a while. I sighed with relief when I heard the shower come on from upstairs. I felt like I had a little bit of time to stretch out and get a little more comfortable. I got up from under the sofa, every bone cracked, I was in so much pain. I did a few stretches until I heard the front door open and I rushed to hide again. I could hear footsteps, but not just any footsteps, Vanessa's footsteps. Her loud, clunky heels were getting closer. I quickly moved the blanket back in place.

"Daniel!" she screamed on the top of her voice before a loud noise was heard. I assumed she threw her bag on the kitchen unit.

"Daniel!" she repeated to shout.

"Hang on Mum!" I heard Daniel shout from upstairs.

I was dreading that conversation, and although in my heart I knew I needed to hear it, nothing could prepare me for *'the truth'*, nothing at all.

Chapter 21
Family Scandal

Vanessa sat for some time on one of the breakfast stools. I had lifted the blanket a little so I could try and make out what was going on. Her hands were clenched tight together. I could just about see her. Eventually Daniel walked in having showered and changed, looking a lot better than he did earlier in the morning. There was a lot of silence, neither of them really knowing what to say.

"You want a drink?" Daniel asked.

"Large." Vanessa said, not even joking. It can't have been later than 8.30am, but obviously the conversation was going to be a difficult one. So Vanessa had a large red wine and Daniel was straight back on the beer. I saw them both almost drink their drink in one mouthful.

"What are we going to do Mum?" Daniel said, with desperation to his voice.

"What's Megan said?" Vanessa asked, calm, collected and in control of her emotions like usual.

"Not much, she's completely turned on me though, she keeps saying that something doesn't feel right."

"Just reassure her that everything is fine. Nothings changed."

"Are you serious! Of course it's changed and if Zoe really is who she says she is then she isn't just going to go away."

"You leave Zoe to me."

"Why didn't you warn me?"

"I didn't want to worry you. I thought I could deal with it without it interfering in your lives. It was that bloody picture you carry."

"What picture?" Daniel asked, suddenly becoming alert.

"The one in your wallet."

"What about it?"

Vanessa paused for a moment. Silence.

"Mum."

"I put one of them with her when I left her that night."

"You did what?!"

"Look, I know we said that she goes with nothing but Daniel, she was a newborn baby. I had just delivered her. I couldn't leave her with absolutely nothing." Vanessa in that moment showed remorse, guilt, maybe even a little love for the baby she chucked away.

"Are you kidding me? So my life, Megan's life, all our fucking lives might fall apart because you decided to give that thing a picture."

"I'm sorry, I didn't know this would happen."

"Yes, well, good job Mother. Now we have a messed up, emotional kid longing for her fucking mother."

"Megan won't believe her."

"And what if she does? I did not want that baby then and I most certainly don't want it now."

"Listen to me. As far as Megan is concerned that baby is dead! Her baby died at birth, we all mourned her, buried her and that's that. Done."

"I wish she had have fucking died."

"Daniel."

"No. Mother. No. This is on you. I trusted you to get rid of it. The only thing I have ever asked you to do for me." Vanessa slammed her wine glass on the kitchen unit, it smashed everywhere. Vanessa stood up.

"Don't you talk to me like that. I gave you everything, everything! You spoiled brat. I will sort it out."

"You better because if Megan ever finds out what we did. I will never forgive you." Vanessa left the kitchen.

I had soaked the floor with all the tears that I had cried listening to what actually happened to me when I was born. I almost felt sorry for Vanessa. It all finally made sense and you know what? Vanessa might have done all the dirty work, but it was Daniel! All of it was Daniel, because he didn't want me. He loathed me, hated me, despised me, he didn't want me messing up his perfect little life, his perfect little world he had created with Megan. He was an absolute monster. Vanessa wasn't innocent, but was she really that bad? She did whatever she could for her son, she did what she thought was best, she did

206

whatever she had to do as a mother. I had all these plans of how I was going to destroy Daniel, how I was going to make him pay. I wanted him to feel the pain I had felt my whole life.

But unfortunately I never got that far...

I waited until the coast was clear before I attempted to leave the house. I felt crippled, honestly my body had never felt so stiff. My arms and legs were all goose-bumped and marked from being on the floor for so long. I could hear Vanessa telling Daniel not to worry at the front door, and so I used the opportunity to quickly leave through the patio doors. It felt so good to be out in the fresh air, even though I was freezing, the sun was starting to rise and I could just about feel the heat on my skin. I felt like I could breathe again. I kept myself close to the house walls as I made my way around the house making sure I wouldn't be seen. I waited in the distance until Vanessa had driven off before I ran, shoes in my hands, past the water fountain and into the trees to get to the bottom of the drive. When I finally got there my feet were dirty and a little bloody from stones, gravel and anything else I might have stepped on. The end of their drive was always very busy with traffic, it was a main road, the house was hidden away and you almost forgot that traffic surrounded it. It was a hidden gem, hiding away from reality. I tried to flag down a taxi but no one was stopping, I didn't blame them.

I bet I looked a right state, I certainly felt it. In the end I switched my phone on and rang a taxi to take me home. I was running out of time. I needed to see Megan and fast.

I couldn't settle back home. I showered and changed into some comfy clothes, pants and a hoodie. I paced my bedsit with my phone in my hand longing to call Sandra, wanting to tell her everything, wanting to tell her that I finally knew the truth. I knew she would know what to say to make me feel better. But talking to Sandra wasn't an option, I hoped she was there with me, just like her letter said. I really needed to talk to Megan on my own, without anyone else there to manipulate the situation. But how? I had loads of missed calls and messages from Vanessa which totally contradicted what I heard her say to Daniel. Vanessa was definitely trying to lure me into a false sense of security.

VANESSA:
Zoe love, I'm not angry, we really need to talk.
Please you're not alone, I panicked, I am so sorry I lied, ring me x
Zoe please, I want to help you.
You still have a job if you want to come to the salon? We really need to talk.

Message after message, she wouldn't give up, she wanted me to trust her, but I wasn't stupid. I had no idea what she was capable of in order to protect her son. She had already gone to extreme lengths for him, I think she would have done anything to me given half the chance. I would not let her hurt me again.

ZOE:
I quit. I know the truth Vanessa. I promise you, you will not get away with this. You or Daniel.

That was the message I sent to Vanessa before blocking her on absolutely everything. That was it. I was done with her. I laid on my bed, looking up to the ceiling. I was the only person in the entire world I could rely on. I was all I had. I remember waiting until 9am the next morning when I sent Megan a message. It took me about an hour to actually send it. I didn't want to sabotage the possibility of talking to her by saying the wrong thing. I got to the point where I didn't think she would find anything I sent right, so I ended up just saying,

ZOE:
Please can I talk to you Megan. I am not a bad person. Please just hear me out.

I never got a response. At 2pm I sent another one.

ZOE:

Megan, I know you're hurting and confused but you cannot trust Vanessa or Daniel. Please talk to me.

No response, 5.30pm.

ZOE:
Me again. I really need to talk to you. Please. I am begging you.

No response. I wondered if she had blocked my number. Then at 7.45pm my phone went off. I hesitated for a moment before looking and finding a message from Megan. I felt sick to the stomach as I read Megan's words to me.

MEGAN:
You are a very sick girl. I hope you get the help you need. Stay the fuck away from me and my family. I wish I had never met you. Consider yourself blocked.

I sobbed. Wow I thought. Vanessa and Daniel had really got inside her head, she actually believed that I was crazy, obsessed, a liar. I wasn't any of those things, well I did lie to get to that point but I was her daughter, she was my mum. Megan needed to know the truth. Maybe it was easier for everyone to pretend like I didn't exist? Vanessa and Daniel had already done it once. Megan thought I was crazy and couldn't even bear thinking about what happened all those years ago, so maybe it suited them all to pretend, to just ignore me and move on with their lives. But where was my closure? Where was my moving on with my life? I had to finish what I started, even though the consequences would be unbelievable.

I left it a few days, locking myself away from the world, eating crap and watching reality tele on my little 22 inch TV that I had invested in a few months before. Anything to distract myself from what was going on in my own head, it wasn't working though, not in the slightest, in fact it was making me feel worse. Somehow I found similarities in everything that I was watching. I turned off the TV and threw the remote on a pile of clothes, sighing out of the window as I did. I didn't know it but I didn't really have time to sit back and do nothing, time was going so fast. If only I knew how fast maybe I could have done more. I guess I will never know.

I decided on that day that this situation, what happened to me, would not define me and dictate my entire life. I was going to start again, move away, a fresh start, perhaps somewhere in the country. I fancied a little village, something that was really picturesque, away from the hustle and bustle of the city. I wanted to work on myself, build something that I could be proud of, don't get me wrong, I was so proud of how far I had come. I loved my little bedsit and the way I had finally made it a home and somewhere I enjoyed spending time, but that was all built and based on lies. I wanted to go somewhere as Zoe, get a job as Zoe and live my life as me. Maybe I could live in a cottage? Maybe near a river? Somewhere I could go and reflect, imagine how peaceful that would be? How relaxing? No Vanessa, Megan, salons, cities, smoke, fog, just fresh country air. I checked my bank account on my phone, I had saved nearly £9000 from the salon. I had gained loads of experience working at the salon that I could add to my CV so I thought I could easily get myself a little job somewhere. I fancied myself as a receptionist in a boutique hotel, or even another small salon. I started to get so excited thinking about my life, my future, my options. I had so much going for me and so much to live for. But I couldn't get too carried away, I couldn't plan too much. I had to speak to Megan! But Megan had blocked me, I couldn't contact her, or could I?

I grabbed my bag from the kitchen and headed into the shopping centre. I was searching for a second hand phone shop, it didn't take me long before I spotted one on the second floor- 'Second Chance'. I was only in there about twenty minutes before I left with a black Motorola flip phone, only costing me £35.00. I knew what I was going to be doing was wrong. But like I have said before, I had no choice and I was really running out of time. I put the SIM in the side of the phone that I had just bought for £2.00 and set the phone up as quickly as I could outside the shop. My hands were shaking with adrenaline but before long, there it was, a second phone all set up with credit on it.

I went and found myself a bench to sit on, holding the phone tight in my hands whilst watching all the everyday people getting on with their lives. I felt like I had gone full circle, sat observing everyone getting on with their day to day routine. I was always longing to be part of something, longing to be part of normality, somehow I didn't think my life would ever be normal. I took my actual phone out of my pocket and scrolled to 'contacts', taking a moment for clarity here and there, because what I was planning was borderline stalking. I scrolled through my contacts and found Megan's number which I added to the new phone. That was it, done. I now had access to Megan, another way in which to contact her. There was no actual guarantee she would even answer. The number wouldn't be recognised and even if she did answer, once she heard my voice, I was sure she would immediately hang up and block me again. It would be a vicious circle.

I had one chance at this. I couldn't mess it up. I bought a takeaway coffee from a kiosk at the shopping centre and went and sat in the park opposite Vanessa's salon. It was 1pm and I could see that it was very busy, the doors were open and clients could be seen going in and out. I sat patiently and waited. I was hoping I would see Megan, perhaps I could have followed her? I could have worked out her routine? I really had no idea but somehow being there made me feel like I was actually doing something. Not much happened, I think I did see Vanessa at one point by the receptionist desk but I wasn't sure. When it got to 5pm, I decided to go home. I walked past The Plant Pot, I did think about going in, but I really wasn't up to seeing Jack, so I went home- alone.

Chapter 22
The End

Nothing had happened. Nothing had changed, weeks had passed. The phone I had bought was put away in it's box because I was too scared to send anything. I went from my bedsit to outside Vanessa's salon and back to my bedsit again. I wasn't eating properly or keeping up with my appearance. I now had roots, really bad roots. I was leaving my hair to wave naturally, I was leaving the house in my comfy joggers and hoodies and I barely wore any makeup. I was starting to become unnoticed again, no one looked at me, smiled at me, really acknowledged me. I wasn't bothered, not at that point, my appearance was the least of my worries.

Megan wasn't ever at the salon it seemed, unless I missed her but I was there, outside of it, most of the time from 8am until late just sitting on that bench. I kept the photo of Megan with me at all times, holding onto it with hope, every time I watched the salon. I kept it under my pillow at night too. I desperately needed to figure out my next moves. I felt like I wasn't getting anywhere. I didn't even have a car so I couldn't even get to Megan's easily. I couldn't just follow her... hang on a minute I suddenly thought. I could get a taxi? I could get a taxi to Megan's? I could try and talk to her when she was alone? Perhaps I did have some options. I rushed to the main road and tried to flag down a taxi in my 'light bulb' moment. It didn't take long before one pulled up for me.

"Walford Hall, Cheshire please." I said, in a rush. I closed the door, put on my seatbelt and sat back in the back-seat, gazing out of the window hoping that everything would be alright.

"Oh Sandra, I wish you were here." I said, under my breath. I wiped a tear from my eye as the taxi got closer to Megan's house. I asked the taxi driver to drop me off at the bottom of the drive to avoid being seen straight away by anybody.

Walking to Megan's, I was terrified but also determined. I ran my fingers through my hair, trying to make myself look a bit more presentable and not like I had been dragged through a hedge backwards. When I got to the water fountain, Daniel's car wasn't on the drive, I knew he would have possibly been at work, but stood there realising this was the moment, this was it, there was no one else here, just me and Megan, it sent shivers through me.

I took the photo of Megan out of my pocket and looked intensely at it before kissing it. I snuck around the side of the house, keeping my body low to avoid being seen. There was a variety of plant pots, hanging baskets, garden ornaments, all different colours, sizes, all holding the most beautiful, exotic, colourful flowers. I hovered my hand over them all and found a small silver, oval shape planter hidden away by some red roses. It caught my attention because it had a small fairy figure sitting in the centre of it. I looked once more at the picture and I hid it with the fairy, placing it inside the fairy's arms. I covered it back with the roses and headed back to the front of the house.

I approached the door with caution, constantly checking over my shoulder, worried that Vanessa would somehow be there and ready to drag me away. Was this too good to be true? I got closer and closer until I found myself so close, I was standing on the silver 'welcome' mat directly outside the main door. I stood small looking up to the black, lion head, door knocker. I took a deep breath, my heart pounding with adrenaline. I reached my sweaty, almost wet dripping hand to the lion and after a few seconds I knocked on the door three times. I let go and felt frozen to the spot. There was no going back now. I waited patiently not taking my eyes off the door. It took a while but eventually I could hear movement at the other side of the door, a few twists and turns of the locks later and it opened. Megan stood gobsmacked to see me. "You have got to be kidding me?" Megan looked like she had seen a ghost.
"Megan. Please." I said, holding the door open with my hands.
"Please, I'm begging you." I pleaded desperately.
"What do you want from me?!"

"Please don't pretend like you haven't thought about it." I said, trying to just talk to her, to reason with her.

"I have got no idea what you're talking about!"

"That you're my mother!"

"You really think I'm your mother!" Megan said, rubbing her face with her hands.

"You are my mother! Vanessa told me that you didn't want me, she told me that none of you wanted me." I was rushing my words, trying to get everything I needed to say out because I could see Megan losing patience with me.

"This is just ridiculous."

"Why would I lie Megan?"

"I can't do this." Megan tried to force the door shut but I used my whole body to stop her.

"The night I told you, I didn't go home. I hid under the sofa, I heard Vanessa and Daniel the next day when you left with Chloe. I heard them."

"Heard them what?"

"I heard Vanessa and Daniel say they had planned the whole thing, Vanessa got rid of me because Daniel didn't want me."

"Get your hands off my fucking door."

"No Megan." I screamed. Megan let go off the door which sent me falling straight into it. Megan paced a few times. I got myself up.

"You expect me to believe that my own husband pretended that our baby was dead. We buried her! You're crazy!"

"You said our baby, but it wasn't was it? It wasn't Daniels! How would I know that?!"

"I must have told you when we were drinking or something!"

"No Megan! You didn't!" We were both screaming and shouting over each other trying to justify what we were saying.

"Vanessa told me about what happened when she discovered who I really was, she's known for months now."

"My daughter is dead."

"You have to believe me! I'm your daughter! I'm your baby!" I could no longer hold back the tears. I felt like I was losing my mind.

"My baby died!!"

"No, it was a lie."

"My daughter died the moment I gave birth to her, I saw her briefly, she wasn't breathing."

"No. No."

"You are not my daughter! My daughter is dead."

"I am. I am her. I am your first baby. It was all a lie. Daniel didn't want to lose you but he couldn't bear the thought of bringing up someone else's baby."

"I got close to you out of pity because I wanted to make you feel better. I told you what happened to me when I was younger and you've come up with this fantasy because you crave a family so badly. I am not your fucking mother. I am not responsible for you!"

"It's true. I am telling you the truth, Vanessa found out and she said she was going to help me tell you, but she lied, just like she's been lying to you for your whole life."

"I will call the police if you don't leave Zoe!"

"I was left in a box on a step in Salford, only hours old. Your little girl, your baby. Megan, please!"

I was emotionally and physically exhausted with trying to get Megan to listen to me, to just hear me out, I was saying everything I needed to but Megan wasn't really listening. I noticed Megan suddenly pause in thought, looking over my shoulder. I slowly turned to find Vanessa standing behind me, dressed head to toe in black like she was about to attend a funeral, she even had the black hat to match. I took a moment to gather my breath.

"Well go on then! Please tell her who I am." I sobbed.

Vanessa looked at me before facing Megan.

"I'm sorry Megan, she did tell me these things." I looked at Megan nodding, Vanessa was going to tell the truth, everything was going to be alright.

"And I did tell her that I would tell you...because I hoped you could convince her to get some help."

I froze on the spot. Vanessa lied again.

"Get out!" Megan screamed in my face.

"Please don't listen to her! She's evil."

"You need to leave you're on private property." Vanessa said, grabbing hold of my hands tight from behind. I had no energy in me to physically try and put up a fight. I felt so defeated.

"You've got to believe me! The picture Daniel carried around with him in his wallet. I've got one exactly the same!" I could feel Vanessa's grip tightening on me as she started to drag me away.

"It's even got writing on the back, Vanessa's writing." I struggled as much as I could with Vanessa, but she was too strong. I was weak and getting weaker by the minute. Megan stopped frantically pacing for a brief second.

"Well go on then, if you've got this picture, show me." she stood hands on hips, looking in complete distress. My eyes lit up.

"It's..." I paused realising I didn't have the picture. Where was it? I couldn't remember.

"For god sake, come with me." Vanessa said. Megan was just laughing in hysterics, thinking I was just bullshitting her.

"No hang on, I put it..."

"I have had enough of this! I have tried to be nice! I have tried to be reasonable, now you're going!" Vanessa said, dragging me backwards so much so that my legs gave way.

"Let go of me!" I used everything I had to fight Vanessa off me and I ran to the side of the house.

"Zoe!!" Vanessa shouted after me.

"Maybe you'll believe me now." I was so determined. I found all the plant pots but I couldn't see my picture. I dug my hands in the soil, pulling out the perfectly grown plants and fresh bulbs, it was nowhere to be seen.

"It was there, it was right there." I cried.

"Zoe come on." Vanessa tried to restrain me once more but I pushed her away running to Megan who was in the distance.

"Megan, it was there! Why wont you believe me?!!" At that point I was literally begging her.

"Zoe! Either you go home or I'm calling the police!" Vanessa said, red in the face.

"She's lying Megan. You are my mother! You are."

"You are wrong! You are so wrong! Now get out!!" Megan grabbed me by my hair and dragged me all around the house. I got a glimpse of Vanessa who seemed shocked at Megan's actions. Megan threw me to the floor, near the water fountain.

"Get away from me you pathetic little freak. I never want to see you ever again! Who would want a daughter like you!" Megan left me, she turned her back on me and went back inside. Vanessa walked past me, looking a little remorseful but more relieved that it was over, she followed Megan inside and closed the door behind her. They had both gone.

Those words, I couldn't get out of my head "who'd want a daughter like you." I almost got up in a daze, those words going round and round in my head. I felt myself walking but I didn't know where to, I was cold, getting colder. It felt damp, I think it had started raining. My head was painful, like I couldn't hold it up much longer. I remember just walking and walking and walking, all of a sudden out of nowhere...

"Zoe! Zoe!" I heard from behind me. Was I dreaming? Who was it? I didn't look and carried on walking, I kept hearing my name. I turned in the darkness, it was foggy all of a sudden. Megan stood staring at me, she held out her arms.

"Baby." That was it, my moment, I ran towards her, my eyes fixated on hers, I felt it, I felt peace.

All of a sudden, bright lights, loud noises. I am slipping away, that's what it feels like. My life is slowly leaving me. I can hear screaming, lots and lots of screaming. I'm not afraid though, I am emotionally exhausted. I need to rest now. Someone is panicking, really panicking. It's cold, ice cold, the type of cold that sends your hands blue. I can't feel my body, not properly, everything around me is really blurry, I can't really make anything out. The sounds are muffled, almost like I am underwater, deep below the surface. I'm consumed by the void darkness trapped within the pit of it's unrelenting bleakness until a sudden, sharp light catches my attention. It's almost too painful to keep my eyes open. I go to shut my eyes but I am locked in it's grasp- moved harshly, jilted, shook with force. I am being held, but they need to let me go now. What happened tonight was always meant to happen and now there is somewhere else I was always meant to be.

My name is Zoe, just Zoe and this is the day I die. I feel numb, cold. My name is being shouted over and over again. My face is getting wetter, drip by drip. The shouting gets louder.

"Go! Go! Get a doctor! Get an ambulance." I can hear panicking.

"I didn't see her, she just ran out." a voice I didn't recognise said.

"Zoe, Zoe! I'm so sorry I didn't believe you. If I would have known the truth, I would have come looking for you. I always wanted you. My baby, I have never got over losing you. I have waited my whole life for this, for you."

Everything is blurry, my vision is going but I can just about make her out, it's Megan.

"The picture." It hurts to move, to talk but I use everything I have left to say my final words to her.

"Yeah you put it with the fairy."

"It reminded me of you."

"We are going to spend so much time together, mother and daughter.

"Mum, I love you." I am losing sight of Megan, but I can feel her holding me tight.

"Zoe! Zoe!" her voice getting quieter, muffled, distorted, everything is slowly fading to black. This is it. The end.

I realised my purpose in life and I fulfilled it, it is my greatest achievement. All I needed to do was to find my mum, that's all I have ever needed. My time spent in this world was not wasted. I was so afraid it wouldn't happen but it did. After eighteen years my mum held me for the very first time. I know I didn't get long with her but trust me it was enough. My story will go unheard and unread by so many people, but the ones that were there, that were involved, will know the truth about me. I hope I live on in Megan and in Chloe, they will keep my spirit alive. I am going to go and find Sandra now, I am sure she is waiting for me somewhere with a round of drinks in. I can only hope Jack knew how I really felt about him, he will go on living his life and one day find the girl of his dreams. I wished it could have been me, I did you know, I did love that boy.

My name is Zoe, just Zoe. The name is actually of Greek Origin and comes from the name Eve, which ironically means life- eternal life. I was eighteen years old when I was hit by a 44 ton lorry, I died at the scene. I was here for a moment and then I was gone. I wish you all a very long and happy life.

Printed in Great Britain
by Amazon

33217881R00129